"I do a lot of things that I didn't do before."

Maddy's voice was full of amusement, but West reacted angrily. "Tell me," he shouted harshly, "did you go out with him?"

"The way you're going on, anyone would think you still cared," Maddy retorted fiercely. "Or is it just that you can't get used to the idea that I don't belong to you anymore?"

His fingers suddenly bit into her wrist, so hard that she had to bite off a gasp of pain. "Yes," he admitted, his voice filled with inner rage and despair. "Yes, God help me, I still care. You're mine! You'll always be mine. And to hell with the divorce." He lunged for her, but Maddy stepped quickly back.

"No!" she cried out in horror. "Can't you understand? I've finished with you!"

SALLY WENTWORTH began her publishing career at a Fleet Street newspaper in London, where she thrived in the hectic atmosphere. After her marriage, she and her husband moved to rural Hertfordshire, where Sally had been raised. Although she worked for the publisher of a group of magazines, the day soon came when her own writing claimed her energy and time. Her romance novels are often set in fascinating foreign locales.

Books by Sally Wentworth

HARLEQUIN PRESENTS

HARLEQUIN ROMANCE

Don't miss any of our special offers. Write to us at the following address for information on our newest releases.

Harlequin Reader Service
901 Fuhrmann Blvd., P.O. Box 1397, Buffalo, NY 14240
Canadian address: P.O. Box 603,
Fort Erie, Ont. L2A 5X3

SALLY
WENTWORTH

driving force

Harlequin Books

TORONTO • NEW YORK • LONDON
AMSTERDAM • PARIS • SYDNEY • HAMBURG
STOCKHOLM • ATHENS • TOKYO • MILAN

Harlequin Presents first edition August 1989
ISBN 0-373-11197-5

Original hardcover edition published in 1988
by Mills & Boon Limited

CHAPTER ONE

'HELLO, Maddy, it's Laura.'

'Why, Laura! Hello. How are you?' There was surprise in Maddy's voice as she answered, and behind the surprise a sharp note of apprehension. It had been more than five months now since her mother-in-law— no, her *ex*-mother-in-law—had last telephoned her, and then it had been a duty call to tell her of West's crash during a race, although Maddy and all the rest of the world had already known of it from the radio and television news.

'I'm well, thank you. And you? Are you still doing your freelance nursing?'

'Why, yes. As a matter of fact you're lucky to have caught me at the flat; I only got back from a job last night.'

'Really? Was it an interesting case?'

'Yes, very.' Maddy tried to put enthusiasm into her voice. 'It was in Wales. Looking after quite a well-known horsewoman who'd fallen and hurt her back.' Put that way, the job sounded quite good, whereas in fact the woman's house had been miles away from anywhere, cold and draughty, and the patient herself bad-tempered and autocratic, treating Maddy more like a general servant than the trained nurse and physiotherapist that she was. It had been a gruelling two months, but Maddy had stuck it out until the

woman was walking again, unlike the two previous
nurses, who'd each stayed only a short time.

But Laura Marriott obviously wasn't very
interested. As soon as Maddy stopped speaking she
said, 'And do you have another job lined up?'

There was a note of eagerness in her tone that immediately made Maddy suspicious and start to
wonder, why the phone call? Laura had blamed
Maddy for the break-up of the marriage, and since
the divorce had only contacted her that once. Now,
when Maddy had first heard her voice, she had felt
a terrible fear that something else had happened to
West, but she knew her ex-mother-in-law well enough
to realise that, if anything had been wrong, Laura
would have come right out and said it; there wouldn't
have been all this polite preamble. But she also knew
that Laura loved organising people, especially if it
meant that she could do someone a favour in the
process. So she said warily, 'I'm having a break at
the moment, but I know the agency has another case
for me.'

Which was a convenient half-truth; she wasn't
booked to go on any specific case, but the agency
always had plenty of work for her.

'I'm glad I've caught you when you're not working.'
Laura Marriott paused, then added rather awkwardly, 'I'm coming up to London myself one day
this week. I wondered if we might meet? Perhaps have
lunch together.'

It was Maddy's turn to hesitate, on the brink of an
outright refusal. There was no way that she wanted
to exchange social chit-chat with West's mother; all
it would do would be to awaken memories she was

trying hard to forget. But then, she didn't think Laura would want to meet *her* socially either, so why the meeting?

As if sensing her thoughts, the other woman said quickly, 'Please don't say no, Maddy. It is rather important.'

'Is it? Can't you tell me over the phone?'

'No, I would much rather meet you. What day will you be free? Tomorrow?'

The urgency in her tone again made Maddy blink in surprise, and she realised that it must be something to do with West; Laura would never have been so eager if she had just wanted her to go and nurse some friend of hers.

'I suppose I could make tomorrow,' Maddy admitted guardedly. 'But I'm meeting a friend at two-thirty,' she added, giving herself an excuse to cut the meeting short if feelings got high.

'Thank you. Perhaps we could meet at the restaurant in Harrods? At twelve-thirty?'

'Yes. All right. Until tomorrow, then.'

Which left just over twenty-four hours for her to wonder just why Laura wanted to see her, Maddy thought as she put down the receiver. And it was only then that she realised that neither of them had once mentioned West's name.

Harrods' window displays were as eye-catching as ever when Maddy walked past them from the Underground the next day. When she'd been married she had had an account with the store and had done a lot of shopping there, but since the divorce most of her shopping was done at local chain stores and supermarkets. Pausing to look at a lay-out of gorgeous evening dresses, Maddy caught sight of her reflection in the window and smiled at herself. A year ago she had been married to West Marriott, the famous racing driver, and had lived and dressed to suit the image. Now that she was just plain Madeline French again, there was a frown of tiredness between her brows and, sometimes, when she was alone, a deep sadness in her eyes. Her clothes were smart, but quite ordinary, and where once commissionaires had rushed to open doors for her and call her by name, now she was sure they wouldn't even notice her.

And she was right; the doorman didn't even glance in her direction as she pushed open the heavy glass doors and walked into the store. Her mouth twisting in cynical amusement, Maddy walked through the shop towards the lifts. She paused at one or two counters, feeling no great anxiety to be on time; her mother-in-law had lost the right to that courtesy as well as everything else when she'd accused Maddy of wrecking her son's life. A display of beautiful belts caught her eye and she fingered one in pale blue leather with a buckle of lapis lazuli, shaped like a butterfly with outspread wings. As West Marriott's wife she wouldn't have thought twice about buying it; now she knew she had nowhere to go to wear anything so flamboyant.

Laura was already there when she arrived, sitting at a table with a drink in front of her. There was a strained look about her eyes, replaced by one of relief when she saw Maddy being led across the restaurant towards her. When she reached the table there was a little moment of awkwardness, neither woman knowing how to greet the other. At length Maddy just

sat down without kissing Laura's cheek as she used
to do, or even shaking hands.

'Thank you for coming. Would you like a drink
while you're deciding what to order?'

'Just a Perrier water, please.' Maddy somehow had
an idea she was going to need her wits about her for
the next couple of hours.

Again she was right. Oh, Laura observed the
niceties, waiting until they'd ordered and been served
before she got down to what she really wanted, filling
the gap by asking about Maddy's family and friends.
But when they were well into their soup, she said, too
casually, 'Aren't you interested in how West is getting
on?' There was also a note of reproach in her voice,
but mostly, Maddy decided, because Laura had had
to bring the subject up herself when she had wanted
Maddy to ask.

'I'm sure you're taking very good care of him,' she
answered, refusing to be drawn.

A little frown of annoyance wrinkled Laura's well-
preserved skin. 'He's having the best of attention, of
course,' she said stiffly. 'His legs are mending quite
well, although...'

'Please,' Maddy broke in sharply, 'I don't want to
hear.'

'Well, really! You were married to him for nearly
four years. Surely you care?'

'It was because I was married to him that I don't
want to hear.' Maddy bit her lip, aware that her voice
had risen in anger. 'Perhaps you'd just better tell me
why you want to see me,' she said bluntly.

Laura looked embarrassed. 'Well—as a matter of
fact, it was about West.'

'What about him?'

The older woman hesitated, then sighed. 'I'm worried about him,' she admitted. 'He—he isn't responding to treatment.' She looked at Maddy, waiting for her to ask why, and when she remained stubbornly silent, Laura Marriott went on, 'As I said, I provide him with the best of care, but he won't take advantage of it.'

There was such a helpless look in her eyes that Maddy relented a little. 'You mean he's refusing to do anything his doctors tell him?'

'Well . . . yes.'

'He always was a terrible patient,' Maddy commented. 'He just hates being ill. I shouldn't worry; he'll heal eventually.'

'I wish that were so,' Laura said on a note that brought Maddy's eyes swiftly to her face. 'He doesn't seem to have any impetus to get well.'

'Not even to get back to the race-track as quickly as possible so that he can try and kill himself again?' Maddy said in bitter sarcasm. 'Oh, surely you must be wrong?'

'No, I'm not wrong. You see, there's no question of him going back to racing. In fact, the surgeons have told him that he might never be able to walk again.

Maddy stared into her eyes for a moment, then looked quickly down at the table, her face as white as the damask cloth. When West had had his accident she had inadvertently caught a replay of it on the television news. She had watched only long enough to learn that he wasn't dead, and then she had closed her eyes and ears to everything else about it. But the actual horror of the crash she couldn't shut out; that, the one thing she had dreaded so much that she couldn't go on living with the fear of it, she had to go on seeing in her mind. Still had to. Slowly she looked up. 'West and I are divorced.' she said tightly.

'I know that. But he's so moody and unhappy. And you know what a short temper he has sometimes. It makes life rather unpleasant for his nurses and they won't stay. I . . .'

'No!'

'Maddy, *please*. I'm absolutely desperate. You know I wouldn't have come to you if I could possibly have found anyone else.'

'No,' Maddy repeated. She began to push her chair back to leave, but a waiter came up and put a plate in front of her, asked her what vegetable she wanted.

Taking advantage of it, Laura reached out and gripped her wrist. 'Please, you must listen to me.'

'I don't have to listen to you,' Maddy answered as soon as the waiter had gone. 'You want me to go and nurse him. Well, I won't. I—I couldn't.'

'What do you mean? Why couldn't you?'

'My God, Laura, I'm a nurse! I've seen the way people end up after they've been in car crashes. I divorced West because I couldn't bear to see him end up like that. How could you possibly expect me to go and look after him?'

'Maddy, I've tried. There's no one else. He seems to—to deliberately send them away.'

'Put him in a private nursing home, then,' Maddy said brutally.

'I tried that. They sent him home within a week,' Suddenly Laura looked very tired. 'I'm at my wits' end. I just don't know what to do. You're my last hope, Maddy. West's last hope.'

'Rubbish! You're—you're being over-melo-dramatic. I'm sure that you could put him in Stoke Mandeville or some other hospital that specialises in accident cases.'

To Maddy's consternation, tears gathered in Laura's eyes, and one trickled down her cheek before she hastily found her handkerchief and dabbed it away. With any other woman, Maddy would have thought that the tears were faked, merely a ploy to arouse her sympathy, but she knew that Laura wasn't the crying kind, that under that soft and rather fragile exterior she was as hard as nails. Now she shook her head and said, 'His doctors have suggested that to West, but he spent three months in hospital after the crash and vowed he'd never go back there. Can you imagine him in such a place? I think it was that that nearly broke his spirit.' Her voice quivered. 'He begged to be brought home, but then they told him he would never race again.'

'Well, I can see how that would kill his spirit,' Maddy broke in drily. 'Racing was all he lived for.'

'He was racing when you married him,' West's mother pointed out.

'You're quite right. But, like every other inexperi-enced female, I thought he loved me more. But men like West never change, do they?'

'No. I found that out with his father,' Laura answered.

Belatedly Maddy remembered that Laura was a widow, West's father having been killed in a mountain-climbing accident over fifteen years ago. She had seldom spoken of her life with her husband, and never, to Maddy, said anything about their personal relationship. Now it made the younger woman wonder how like his father West was. She ate some of the food on her plate, trying to give the strained atmosphere time to ease a little before saying, 'I'm sorry, Laura, I can't do it. And surely you must see that I'm the last person who ought to look after West, anyway? We didn't exactly part on the best of terms. A patient needs a calm and restful atmosphere in which to get well. With me there, there would be too much tension, too many fights and arguments.'

'But maybe that might be good for him. Even— even hate is a great reason for wanting to live, Maddy.'

Her daughter-in-law gave her a look of angry affront. 'So I'm to be West's whipping-boy, am I?'

'No. I'm sorry, I didn't mean it like that.' Laura reached across the table to touch her in a gesture of contrition. 'I'm just so desperate, Maddy. And I can't just—just stand by and watch him—watch him die.' Her voice broke, and she had to use her handkerchief again.

'Surely he isn't that bad?' Maddy asked in shocked disbelief.

'But he is.' There was the sincerity of despair in Laura's voice. 'He just doesn't want to live as a—as a cripple.'

Maddy gave her time to recover and start pretending to pick at the food before she said, 'Laura, look, what you're doing is emotional blackmail. Have you bothered to think of what your suggestion means to me? How humiliating it would be for me? You know how damn arrogant West can be sometimes, how cold and sarcastic, especially when he thinks he's right.'

'Perhaps he is,' Laura admitted, which was quite something in itself, 'but does any of that really matter when it's a question of trying to save his life?'

She spoke fiercely, her eyes holding Maddy's in intense pleading. But again the younger woman shook her head, although there was doubt in her eyes now that Laura was quick to play on. 'Please, Maddy,' she pleaded. 'Couldn't you just try? If it doesn't work out—well, at least I'll know that I've done everything in my power for him.' She hesitated, then said, 'I haven't spoken about money because I didn't think it came into it, but of course I'll give you any...'

'It doesn't,' Maddy broke in sharply.

'Then *please*, Maddy. He's my son and I can't let him pine away. He *needs* you. If you ever loved him...'

Her face white, Maddy raised dangerously challenging eyes to meet Laura's. 'Oh, no,' she said in low fierceness, 'don't use that one on me. You *know* I loved him so much that I couldn't bear to see him killed. And now you want me to go and watch him die!' Suddenly, pushing back her chair, Maddy snatched up her bag and hurried out of the restaurant, unable to bear any more, almost running in her haste to get away.

She walked aimlessly for a long time, gazing blindly in shop windows, unable to put Laura's pleas out of her mind. She must be exaggerating, Maddy decided. West wasn't the kind of man to just lie in a bed and pine away. His was a strong, indomitable spirit; and even though she thought his bravery misguided, he was still one of the most courageous men she knew.

To get in a car that wasn't much more than an enveloping petrol tank and drive at two hundred miles an hour round a twisting, narrow track with other cars jostling all around you, that took real guts. Maddy shivered convulsively, remembering all the races she had watched in the early years, until she had given up pretending to enjoy them, given up trying to hide her fear because it was making her bitchy and ill, and had refused to go any more.

That was when West had started to lose his temper with her, unable to understand the change in her. He had even offered to let her start the family she so desperately wanted, and had been furious when she had laughed in his face. Gradually then they had become more cold and withdrawn towards one another, although with West there was always seething anger beneath the surface, threatening to erupt, but more often emerging as sadistic scorn. As it had when she had tried to move into a separate bedroom. Maddy shuddered anew at the thought of that night, at the way she had fought him when West had taken her with such a furious domination, but then her body had betrayed her and it had turned into the most sexually satisfying night they had spent together in months. And perhaps that was why West could never understand why she had walked out on him the next morning and refused ever to go back.

When Maddy eventually went back to the flat the phone was ringing. She let it go on until it stopped, and then took the receiver off the hook. She had too much to think about for interruptions, and also she had the nasty suspicion that it might be Laura trying to change her mind. Her mother-in-law was nothing if not tenacious. After making herself a strong cup of coffee, Maddy sat in the big armchair in the sitting-room, so deep in thought that she didn't even notice when the room grew dark.

The trauma of the divorce had gone very deep, especially as West had refused to give his consent. At first he had tried everything to make her go back to him, overriding even his hurt pride to do so. But he had finally accepted that she would never live with him while he continued to race, and eventually he had given in. But those long months while she had waited for him to come to terms with it had been a terrible strain, to say the least, and she was only now beginning to build up some kind of new life for herself. Not that it was much of a life at the moment. She had refused to take a penny from West, even though the alimony offer he had made had been more than generous, but she felt that she should never have married him in the first place, so it was hardly fair to let him keep her after she'd left him.

She had put her name down at the agency and for quite a long time she'd lived out of suitcases, with most of her possessions in store. But after a few months she'd realised that she had to have some sort of base, and had managed to put the deposit on a tiny flat in north London. It was her home now, a place to live in between jobs and a haven if she were ever ill—or even for when she retired. At only twenty-six, Maddy hadn't actually looked that far ahead, but, as she had no intention of marrying again, the time would eventually come.

As she looked round her small sitting-room, furnished with taste and attention to detail, Maddy couldn't help comparing it with High Beeches, the beautiful house in Surrey that West had inherited from his father. His mother had her own flat in St John's Wood, but she had often come to stay, and as she had many friends in the area she had often entertained there. But she had always been good about it, making a point of asking Maddy's permission first—not that Maddy had ever felt in a position to refuse, even if it was inconvenient for her. No, she had been happy in the luxurious house with its six bedrooms, indoor pool—and the huge garage block where West housed his cars. Until things had started to go wrong. Now the thought of going back to that house made her feel sick inside.

And everyone knew they were divorced. It had been in all the papers. What would their friends and relations think if she went back there—even as West's nurse?

Agitatedly, Maddy got to her feet, switched on the light and went over to the windows to draw the curtains. But she paused for a moment, looking down into the street at the cars going by below. One pulled into a space almost opposite and a man got out, tall and fair-haired, and so like West that for a moment her heart lurched. But it wasn't West of course, because West would never drive a car again, never walk briskly across the pavement and run up the steps of the house opposite as this man was doing. It was in that moment that Maddy admitted what in her heart she had known all along. That she would have to try and help him. That she would never be able to live with herself if she didn't try. And she owed West that much—for taking four years out of his life.

Maddy closed the curtains, and, as she went into the kitchen, remembered that Laura had said West needed her. She hadn't felt needed, not really needed, for a long time, especially by West. Oh, she had at first, when they'd been engaged and newly married, but gradually things had changed until she felt that he only needed her for his sexual satisfaction. Although he didn't even need her for that, really; Maddy knew that there were always plenty of women willing to make themselves available to him. Whether he ever took advantage of the offers Maddy didn't know, but she didn't think he had, not while they'd been married; he had always come home too eager to take her to bed for that.

And now, would he ever be able to make love to a woman again? Maddy didn't know, she had made sure that she never found out the extent of his injuries. But now it seemed that she was going to, after all. She put the phone back on the hook and waited for it to ring, sipping another cup of coffee and wondering why she was going to allow her life to be devastated all over again.

It was less than a quarter of an hour before the phone rang. Maddy let its insistent tones fill the flat before she picked it up and said hello.

'Hello, Maddy, it's Laura again. I—I phoned to apologise to you. I didn't mean to upset you at lunch time.' She paused and then said, 'No, that isn't true. I'm not really sorry. I had to try and persuade you, for West's sake.'

'Did he know that you were going to ask me to look after him?'

Laura paused and Maddy could imagine her trying to decide what was best to say. There was a note of truth in her voice when she finally said, 'No. No, I didn't tell him.'

'I didn't think he would ever have allowed you to ask me,' Maddy commented wryly. 'I'm the last person he'd want near him.'

"You might just be that,' Laura retorted tiredly with a flash of her old pride.

'You do realise that he will utterly resent me, don't you?'

Laura gave a little gasp. 'Does that mean that you'll come? Oh, Maddy, I can't thank you enough! I . . .'

'Wait! It only means that I'll consider it. First I want to talk to his doctor, find out if he really is as bad as you say. And it may be that he needs a more specialised nurse than I am.'

'But you're a trained nurse and physiotherapist. Surely that combination is ideal for him?'

'It may be. But I still want to talk to his doctor before I commit myself. Can you arrange that? I shall be home for the whole of this week.'

'Yes, I'll contact him first thing in the morning.'

There was a bubbly note of relief and excitement in Laura's voice that made Maddy envy her optimism. She seemed so sure that she was the right person to look after West, but Maddy was far from sure herself. If anything, she thought it might be the worst arrangement possible—for both of them. 'You won't say anything to West about this, will you?' she cautioned. 'Remember, it isn't definite.'

Laura agreed to this readily enough and rang off after promising to phone again the next morning.

Maddy, who had felt tired to death after her difficult nursing case and longing for a good rest, spent a very sleepless night. But her mother-in-law must have been as persuasive with West's doctor as she had been with Maddy, because she rang quite early the next morning to say that she had arranged an appointment with the doctor in charge of his case that very afternoon. Her eyebrows rose when Maddy wrote down the name of his surgeon; it was a very well-known man in Harley Street, no less.

At ten to three, Maddy strode down the street of Georgian houses, each with half a dozen brass nameplates by the door, fully determined to refuse to look after West if she found Laura had been exaggerating, or if some other nurse could be found for him. She didn't intend to put herself through hell again if there was the remotest possibility of avoiding it.

But after only a few minutes with the surgeon Maddy had to accept that there was no alternative. They stood together looking at the back-lit X-rays of West's hips and legs. They had been broken in so many places that they seemed now to be more metal than bone. The surgeon didn't know that she was West's ex-wife, he thought she was only a nurse, and he began to list the injuries in a detached, clinical manner. And for this Maddy was grateful; it helped her to fight off the ghastly feeling of nausea at this evidence of West's shattered body. His body that she'd loved so much.

'His right arm was broken, too,' the doctor added. 'That's mended now. But it made things difficult for him in hospital.'

'Will he ever walk again?' Maddy asked bluntly.

He shrugged. 'It's highly unlikely.'

'But it's not impossible?' Maddy insisted.

'No, not impossible.' He turned to look at her. 'Given a great deal of the right treatment—and the will to walk again.'

'And does he have it?'

'Not at the moment. Even if he managed to walk, he would never be able to race again. I had to tell him that; he demanded to know.'

'Yes, he would want the whole truth.'

'You know him, then?' he asked in surprise.

Maddy gave the ghost of a smile. 'Yes, I know him.'

'He won't be an easy patient,' the surgeon warned. 'He doesn't want to be helped.'

'But he can't want to stay a cripple.'

'No.' He hesitated, eyeing her. Making up his mind, he said, 'Quite frankly, I think he would rather have died in the crash. And I think that's what he wants to do now.'

'Do you think that I can help him? That anyone can?'

'You're certainly well qualified to do so. Although whether he'll let you or not...' He left the sentence unfinished. 'But if you can it will be well worth while. He's quite a man. But he'll make it damn hard for you,' he warned again. 'He'll try and get rid of you just as he's got rid of all his other nurses and physios. But as you already know him, it might help.' She was silent, looking at the X-rays, and he said curiously, 'Will you take on his case?'

Maddy gave a small sigh, but then nodded decisively. 'Yes, I'll take it. Perhaps you could advise me on the best way to treat him.'

The surgeon gave her an appraising look and began pointing at the X-rays again, telling her which part of West's legs and body were still weak, which beginning to mend.

When she got back to the flat, Maddy rang Laura straight away. The phone was answered at once by Laura herself.

'Yes, all right,' Maddy said. 'I'll come and look after him.'

'Oh, thank God! When will you come—tomorrow?'

'No,' Maddy answered firmly. 'I need a couple of days. He won't get any worse in two days, Laura,' she added before the other woman could protest. 'I'll come down on Friday.'

'I'll send the car for you.'

'No, I have my own car. I'll be there about eleven.'

'All right. And thank you again, Maddy. You don't know how much this means to me,' Laura said in heartfelt sincerity.

'You'd better keep your thanks until you know whether I can help him. He'll probably refuse to let me into his room, let alone treat him,' Maddy told her grimly.

'Oh, Maddy. I just hope and pray...' Laura's voice faltered, but then rallied as she said, 'Shall I tell him that you're coming?'

'I shouldn't. Not until the last minute, anyway. But I'll leave it up to you. Do what you think best.'

That night Maddy took a sleeping pill, determined to get the rest she needed, and spent the next day checking her physio equipment and replenishing what creams and other things she needed. On Thursday she gave herself a day off to go and have her hair done, to spend some of her wages on a few new clothes, to go to a theatre. In other words, to make herself feel that there was something else to life other than work, even if it was only for one day.

She set off just after nine the next morning, avoiding most of the rush-hour traffic, her equipment safely stowed in the small van that she'd bought for the purpose. She reached High Beeches just before eleven and vainly tried to kill the wave of deeply painful emotion she felt when she saw the house again. It's just a case, she told herself. Just another case. You must be detached and unsentimental.

But it could never be just another case, Maddy realised as she drew up and looked at the windows, wondering if West was able to look out and see her, and what his emotions were as he waited.

Laura had been looking out for her and came hurrying to meet her. She wanted to take Maddy to see West at once.

'Does he know I'm coming?'

Laura hesitated, then shook her head. 'No, I—I just told him that a new nurse was arriving today.' She gave an unhappy smile. 'It was cowardly of me, I know, but...'

'It doesn't matter. Maybe it's better this way.' Maddy looked up at the windows. 'Can he see us? Which room have you got him in?'

'Why, his own bedroom, of course. Your——' She hesitated, realising what she was saying. 'The room you used to share with him,' she finished lamely.

Maddy's face tightened and she involuntarily glanced up at the windows in a gable on the right of the house, but Laura said, 'He can't see us. He's in bed.'

Pulling herself together, Maddy picked up one of her suitcases and went to walk into the house, but then remembered that it wasn't her house any more, and she stood back so that Laura could lead the way.

'I've put you in the room next to West's,' Laura said awkwardly. 'It means sharing his bathroom, but . . .'

'It doesn't matter. That will be the best arrangement. And I'll use that dressing-room between the two rooms for my physio equipment. I'll need help taking it up there, though. It needs two people to carry it.'

'I'll get Sandy to help you.'

'Sandy? Is he still here?'

'Why, yes. He doesn't do much work in the garage now, of course. But he helps look after West. Does all the—the personal things for him.'

Which was most welcome news; Maddy had been sure that one of the biggest obstacles she would have to overcome would be West's refusal to let her carry out the more intimate duties that nursing a patient required. But with West's old mechanic to do that, she might stand a chance.

'Shall I take you to see him now?'

'No, there's plenty of time. I'll get my equipment installed and unpack first. Then maybe we could have lunch and a chat about West. And perhaps I could have a word with Sandy. I think it's important that I know as much about his case as I can before I—before I see him.'

Maddy was prevaricating, she knew, putting off seeing West again until the last possible moment, but even as she unpacked and told Sandy where to put her equipment, she wondered if she was wasting her time. If West refused to let her nurse him then there was nothing she could do about it; she would just have to pack everything up again and go. Unless he was in such a weakened state that she could browbeat him into accepting her. There was that possibility of course, although she'd never been able to browbeat him before, and she knew that he would hate her for taking advantage of his weakness. But he already hated her, so that made little difference.

Laura was more forthcoming now that Maddy had committed herself, but there was little more to learn than the doctor had told her. Sandy could probably have told her more, but when Maddy tried to talk to him after he'd taken up West's lunch, she found him polite but unhelpful. She was surprised at first, because they'd got on well enough in the past, but she soon realised that he, too, blamed her for the divorce. She didn't press him any further; to do so would only make him feel disloyal to West and antagonise him more.

Turning to Laura, he said, 'I'll go up and fetch his lunch tray in about half an hour, then.'

'No, that's all right. I'll do it,' Maddy broke in, knowing that she couldn't put it off any longer. But she saw the frown in Sandy's eyes and added placatingly, 'Maybe later we could work out a routine between us?'

He nodded and went away, and Maddy excused herself and went up to her room, where she changed

into white jeans, quite tight ones, and a thin-knit V-
necked sweater that didn't exactly hide her figure. She
never wore a starchy uniform, whoever she was
nursing, unless the patient insisted on it, because she
felt ordinary clothes were more cheerful. And right
now she was going to meet the man she'd been married
to for four years, and there was no way she wasn't
going to look her best, even if he was ill. So she re-
did her face, taking care to accentuate the deep blue
of her eyes that West had so often said he could drown
in—and brushed her dark brown hair until it glowed
about her head.

Maddy stepped back to look at herself in the mirror
for a moment, then, her limbs trembling, she crossed
to the door of West's room, took a deep breath and
gently opened it. He hadn't heard her. He was lying
in the bed, propped up on pillows and facing the
window, but the window was too high and all he could
see were the tops of trees swaying in the breeze outside,
yet his eyes were fixed on them in desolate intentness,
like a man looking through the bars of a prison.
Maddy stood and stared at him in utter shock. She
had been prepared for him to look ill, but never this.
West had a lean, hawklike face that always reminded
Maddy of an Indian chief, of Cochise or Geronimo,
although his hair, instead of being black, was a thick
white blond. But now all the flesh had gone from his
bones, leaving his eyes like grey pools of molten lead
in his shrunken face. Lead where once they had been
bright steel. Dead and hopeless. Not despairing, just
devoid of any emotion.

A terrible surge of love and pity ran through her,
and Maddy wanted to run to him, to hold and comfort

him. Almost she did so, but it suddenly came to her that that wasn't the way to win the battle for West's life. She must be exactly the opposite: hard and scathing; scornful and cold. He hated her already, and if feeding on that hate would make him well again, then hate it would have to be. Her chin lifting in resolve, Maddy stepped through the door, closed it behind her and said coolly, 'Hello, West.'

CHAPTER TWO

Maddy was sure that Sandy would have told West about her, but it was immediately obvious that he hadn't. West's surprise was total. He turned his head sharply to stare at her, stunned disbelief in his eyes. He closed them for a few moments, tightly, then opened them. Lifting his hand, he put it to his mouth, his jaw rigid, his eyes following her as she walked over to the bed. Slowly he took his hand away, then found his voice. 'What the hell are *you* doing here?' he demanded in fierce contempt.

'Didn't they tell you? I'm your new nurse,' she answered calmly, and picked up his wrist. It was very thin, making her heart contract again, but she felt his racing pulse before he jerked his arm away.

'*You?*' he exploded. 'No, you're damn well not!'

'Why not? You need a nurse and I need a job.'

'Well, you can find one somewhere else. You're not going to look after me.'

'You're too late,' Maddy returned calmly. 'I've already been hired.' Going over to a nearby table where all his medicines were set out, she began to go through them.

'Take the money,' West bit out. 'Take it and go.'

'Good heavens,' Maddy remarked. 'Do you really still have to take all this stuff? Anyone would think you were still in hospital.'

28

West's voice rose menacingly. 'You heard me. Get away from here, I don't want you.'

'No.'

'Damn you, Maddy. I don't want your pity.'

'Good, because you're not going to get it. And I'm not leaving.'

'Yes, you damn well are.'

'Oh, really? Who says so?'

'I do, of course.'

'And just how are you going to make me leave? Are you going to pick me up and throw me out?' she asked tauntingly.

He stared at her, his gaunt face taut, his eyes full of angry frustration. Maddy felt herself start to shake again but desperately tried to control it, putting her hands behind her to grip the window sill.

'I can make you leave,' West told her scornfully. 'I can make your life so much hell that you'll be glad to go.'

She laughed. 'You already did that. Remember? It won't work a second time.'

A look of stunned surprise came into his eyes, to be replaced by a grim mask. 'You won't last more than a couple of days.'

'Bet you I will,' Maddy retorted. 'Bet you I last . . . what's the record? How long did the most patient nurse last?'

'Ten days,' West answered reluctantly.

'OK. I bet you I last more than ten days.'

'And if I win?'

Maddy laughed again. 'You won't.'

'Yes, I damn well will,' he said violently.

'Well, in that case you'll have won your prize, won't you? You'll be rid of me. But if I win—*when* I win,' she corrected, '*then* I'll name my prize.'

'How can you expect me to take the bet if you don't name the penalty?'

'But you don't expect to lose, so that can hardly worry you, can it?'

He looked at her suspiciously for a moment, then tiredly turned his head away. 'Get away from here, Maddy,' he said shortly. 'Don't make things worse than they already are.'

Looking at the tautness of his face, she judged that he'd had enough for now, so she walked over to his lunch tray which she saw was hardly touched.

'Finished with this?'

'Yes.' He said it challengingly, and Maddy guessed that Laura and his other nurses had tried to cajole and persuade him to eat.

'Suit yourself. The dogs are going to get fat.'

Picking up the tray, she went to the door and opened it. As she turned to back out with the tray, she glanced at West and their eyes met. For a moment his gaze seared into hers, full of hate and hurt, and an agony of torment. Quickly Maddy turned away, unable to bear it. She managed to shut the door, but had to lean against it for several minutes until her trembling limbs were steady enough to carry her.

Laura was waiting anxiously in the hall. 'Well?' she demanded as soon as they went into the kitchen

'He wants me to leave. He refuses to let me nurse him.'

A defeated look came into the older woman's eyes and her shoulders sagged. 'I see.'

'But I'm not going,' Maddy added tersely as she slammed down the tray. 'I'm going to make him get well whether he likes it or not!'

Laura lifted her head to stare at her, then suddenly began to laugh and cry all at the same time. 'Oh, Maddy. Oh, my dear.' And she took hold of Maddy's hands and gripped them hard.

Madeline, too, began to laugh and gave Laura an impulsive hug, something she had never done when she and West had been married.

Wiping her eyes, Laura said, 'I think this calls for a celebration. Let's have a drink.' They went into the sitting-room, and as Laura poured the drinks she said, 'You're the one ray of hope I've had since I heard that West had survived the crash.'

They began to talk as woman to woman, their old relationship that had made them wary of one another a thing of the past. But after only about ten minutes or so they were interrupted by a buzzer that sounded loudly throughout the house.

'Oh, that's West. He needs something.' Laura jumped to her feet.

'Sit down. Don't worry.'

'You'll go?' Laura sat down again.

'Yes. Presently.' And Maddy talked on until the buzzer sounded impatiently again and Laura looked at her anxiously.

'Aren't you going to go up to him?'

Maddy shook her head. 'Invalids are like children, Laura. They think that the world should revolve round them, and that if they want something they should get it instantly. It's all they have to think about, you see. I'll go up and see what West wants, but in my time, not his.'

But after only a few minutes West put his finger on the buzzer and held it there. A grim look came into Maddy's eyes, but she went up to his room.

'What do you want?' she demanded briskly.

West took his finger from the buzzer, a triumphant gleam in his shadowed eyes. 'Not you, for a start,' he answered harshly.

'OK.' She turned to go out of the door.

'Wait!'

She paused and turned to face him again. 'Changed your mind?' she mocked.

West's jaw tightened. 'Send Sandy up to me.'

'All right. In future, if you want me you buzz once, and for Sandy twice.'

'I'll ring as often as I damn well want.'

'In which case I shall disconnect the buzzer and you won't get anyone until we feel like coming up, will you?' Maddy told him sweetly. She looked around the room. 'And tomorrow we're going to start making some changes in here.' With which parting shot she walked out of the room.

Sandy was over in the garage block, washing West's Ferrari, which had only the thinnest layer of dust on its gleaming red surface. It was a pointless task; West would never drive it again, and he wouldn't let anyone else near it, but Maddy carefully kept this thought out of her face and voice as she told Sandy that West wanted him.

When Sandy came down from West's room half an hour later, Maddy called out to him from the sitting-room where she was sitting at the desk, a large pad of paper in front of her. She smiled at him. 'Shall we work on the timetable now?'

He did so grudgingly at first, but Maddy kept to as much of their present routine as possible and he began to thaw a little. 'I get him up every morning at eight-thirty' he told her. 'Then Mrs Marriott takes him up his breakfast, or if she's away Mrs Campbell gets it ready and I take it up.'

Mrs Campbell was the housekeeper who'd been with the family for years, even longer than Sandy had been West's mechanic. During their marriage, though, she had gone to live in semi-retirement in the nearby village of Uxton, but had maintained her links with the family by coming in to help whenever they entertained and by looking after the house when they were away. But now it seemed that Mrs Campbell was working there almost full-time again, although she wasn't at the house today.

'I take him his lunch,' Sandy went on. 'And afterwards I—er—look after him, and sometimes I sit with him a bit. Then in the evenings, before dinner, I give him a blanket bath and I...'

'You do?' Maddy broke in in surprise. 'Good heavens, Sandy, I didn't know you were so versatile! Where did you learn to do that?'

'One of the nurses taught me,' he answered grimly. 'West couldn't stand the woman near him. He said she'd learnt her nursing with the Spanish Inquisition.' Maddy laughed and he gave a reluctant grin. 'So since then I've always done it for him.'

'He's very lucky to have you,' she said warmly.

He shrugged, and there was a challenge in his Scots burr as he said, 'West doesn't want anyone but me near him.'

Maddy's eyes held his. 'No—but then I'm not just anyone, am I, Sandy?' She didn't wait for him to answer but went on briskly, 'So who takes West his dinner?'

'Mrs Marriott usually takes it up and has hers with him. Then she might stay the evening, or I'll sit with him and then get him ready for the night.' He paused, then added heavily, 'Sometimes he doesn't want anyone with him. And of course, if he wants me during the day, I'll go up and see to him. And if there's no nurse here I'll go up a couple of times in the night and turn him over.'

'So you're more or less on call twenty-four hours a day! Well, that won't do. You must be exhausted. Just because you live over the garage block doesn't mean that you're permanently available. You're entitled to *some* time off.'

He began to argue, but Maddy was adamant. 'West's got to try and learn to be independent,' she insisted. 'If he knows that you'll come running whenever he wants anything, he'll never do anything for himself. It's a case of being cruel to be kind. We've *got* to shake him out of his apathy, Sandy.' He didn't look very convinced, so she said, 'Do you really want to go on looking after cars that he might never drive?'

'He'll get well,' Sandy protested. 'It's only a matter of time.'

'No, he won't. He's given up. Surely you've seen that? And if he doesn't come out of it soon, he's just going to lie there until he gets some illness he won't fight, and then he'll die.'

He gazed at her, then nodded. 'Aye, maybe you're right. I've been hoping against hope. It's not like him to give up.'

So between them they worked out a new routine, and Maddy made Sandy promise that he would stick to it rigidly at least for the first week. 'No going up to West the minute he rings,' she warned. 'If he really needs you I'll let you know.'

'All right.' He grimaced. 'It will make a change to get a full night's sleep.'

When he'd gone, Maddy went into West's study, which was right underneath his bedroom, took out his typewriter and began to type out the timetable, banging the keys as loudly as she could. The buzzer sounded almost immediately, one long, imperious ring.

Remembering how they'd often communicated when they were married, Maddy picked up the receiver of the phone on West's desk and pressed the internal button, knowing that he had a phone beside his bed. After a few moments he answered and said tersely, 'Get up here.'

'Why? What do you want?'

'I have something I want to say to you.'

'Say it now, then.'

'You heard me, come up here at once.' And he slammed down the receiver.

Maddy turned the radio on quite high and went on typing, doing so while the buzzer sounded in her ears for a good five minutes. Then she went up to West's room, humming a tune as if she hadn't a care in the world.

West was sitting up higher in the bed, his thumb pressed firmly on the buzzer, an angry snarl on his face. Still humming, Maddy calmly followed the wires of the electric buzzer to the socket and pulled out the plug, then she went out of the room.

'Wait, damn you!'

West's furious voice followed Maddy down the stairs, but she ignored it and thanked her stars that Laura had gone out to do some shopping. She began typing again, pounding the keys of West's old manual machine, waiting for the internal phone to ring. It did so at last, but she'd had to start on a second copy of the timetable before West finally succumbed to his angry curiosity.

'What the hell are you doing in my study?' he demanded.

'Typing.'

'I know that! You have no right to be there.'

'But your mother said I could go wherever I liked,' she pointed out smoothly.

'I don't give a damn what Laura said. This is my house, not hers, and I don't want *you* in any part of it.'

'Don't you want to know what I'm typing?'

'No, I don't,' he answered tightly, and Maddy could imagine the contained fury in his gaunt face. But anger was a good emotion, it might make him want to fight.

'Well, you'll see it anyway. What were you buzzing for?'

'To tell you to get out of my study. Out of my house, and out of my life! You don't belong in any of them.'

'Perhaps not. But we've already established that you can do nothing about it, so what's the point in going over it again?' Maddy told him with brutal bluntness. 'So if that's all . . .'

'No.' She heard his breath, heavy with impotent bitterness. 'I can't rest with all that row going on. Turn off the radio and stop typing.'

'Why do you want to rest? It's the middle of the afternoon. Why don't you read, or watch the television, or something?'

'Because I don't damn well want to! Now turn it off.'

'No. Just because you want to shut the world out doesn't mean that I have to. This is good music, you ought to listen to it.'

'Don't tell me what I ought to do. Tell my mother I want to see her.'

'Sorry, she's gone out. And Sandy's getting some rest, before you ask. Don't you think they deserve some time off from the chore of looking after you?' And she put the phone down on his silence.

When she'd finished typing, Maddy stayed in the study with the radio on and wrote a letter to her parents to let them know where she was and that her being at High Beeches was for purely professional reasons. Her mother, especially, had been very unhappy about the divorce, and she didn't want them getting any ideas about her and West's getting back together. The letter finished, Maddy found an envelope and addressed it but couldn't find a stamp, so started looking through the drawers of the desk. One of them near the bottom was stuck, but she managed to take the one above it out, and found that the stand of a silver photograph frame, face-down in the drawer, had stopped it from opening. Slowly Maddy reached out to pick up the frame, knowing what it contained even before she turned it over. It was their wedding photo—not an official one, but a shot taken by a friend in an unguarded moment when they had been looking into each other's eyes, their faces full of love, their heads high in the confidence of their enduring happiness.

Maddy gripped the frame very hard, then quickly replaced it in the drawer and shut it away. So much for hope and confidence, she thought bleakly. Tears came to her eyes but she blinked them angrily back; she had given up crying for West long ago, and she wasn't about to start again now. She glanced at her watch; in another half-hour she would go up to him.

He was lying on his back, his eyes closed. Most of the pillows were on the floor, thrown there in a rage, Maddy guessed. Ignoring the pillows, she went over to the medicine table and measured out a dose of the antibiotics that he still had to take, ticking off a chart pinned to the wall that some other nurse had left.

'I know you're awake,' she said, as she stood beside the bed.

West opened his eyes and looked at her malevolently. 'So it wasn't a nightmare.'

''fraid not,' she returned cheerfully. 'I'm quite real.'

'Do you always leave your patients unattended for so long?'

'Depends entirely on the patient. If they need me then I stay around.'

'*I* don't need you. You're the last person I'd ever need.'

It was spoken with such undisguised venom that for a moment Maddy's guard almost slipped. She caught her breath, but managed to cover it by saying quickly, 'It's time for your medication.'

'I don't want it.'

'Ah! Diddums,' she said with mock sweetness. 'And shall I sing you a lullaby tonight?'

West glared at her murderously, dragged himself up and grabbed the medicine glass from her to drink it down.

Turning away so that he couldn't see her face, Maddy busied herself with picking up the pillows and putting them behind his back. 'Do you need anything else?'

'No.' She went to leave, but when she reached the door West said tersely, 'Why have you come here?'

'I told you, I needed a job.'

'Don't give me that rubbish.' He studied her for a moment, then said sourly, 'It doesn't matter; I know why you're here.'

'Do you? I hardly think so.'

He laughed suddenly, a harsh, jarring sound that made Maddy feel suddenly icy cold. 'Oh, yes. Your coming here is your way of saying "I told you so". You were always warning me that I'd crash one day, and now that I have you've come here to gloat, to show me just how right you were.' Maddy gasped, but, before she could speak, West's scornful voice gibed at her again. 'Well, how does it feel to see me like this? Does it give you satisfaction to know that I'll never be able to race again? That's what you always wanted, wasn't it? For me to give it up. Are you enjoying twisting the knife in the wound? Having me lying here in your power? Well, are you, you sadistic little bitch? Are you?'

Hot rage ran through her and Maddy took a hasty step towards the bed, but she saw West's expectant eyes and realised in time that he had deliberately set out to make her angry. She stopped, and smiled grimly. 'Nice try. But you're out of practice. You used to be far more subtle than that when you wanted to hurt.'

His brows flickered for a moment and he lay back. 'You've changed.'

'If you mean that you can't hurt me any more, then yes, I have.' She looked at his averted profile, wondering if he really believed that she'd come there out of some twisted kind of vindictiveness. 'If I'd wanted to gloat,' she said carefully, 'I could have gone to see you in hospital, soon after you crashed.'

West turned to look at her, and his mouth twisted into a cynical smile that looked appalling on his fleshless face. 'Ah, but if you'd come at once it might have looked as if you were worried about me. As if you still cared. And you most certainly didn't want me or anyone else to think that, did you? No, five months is nicely timed for me to know that you're only here out of spite.'

Maddy opened her mouth to tell him that even now it was almost more than she could bear to see him so badly hurt, but then closed it firmly. Now was most definitely not the time. Not if hating her was going to make him start fighting. She turned away, realising that there might never be a time. Going over to the television, she switched it on. 'I think there's some cricket on, the Test Match from Australia.'

'I don't want to watch it.'

'Too bad,' Maddy said heartlessly, and grabbed the remote control before he could reach it. Calculatingly, she put it on a table just a few inches out of his reach, so that if he really wanted to he could manoeuvre himself into a position where he could eventually grab it and turn the set off. But to do so he would have to use his arms to move himself and twist his body to reach out. And if he could do that...

He cursed her as she went out of the room, but Maddy closed the door and went noisily down the stairs—then crept back up to listen breathlessly outside his room. She had turned the television up quite high, so she could hear no other sounds, and after a quarter of an hour she began to give up hope. Maybe he had got interested in the cricket, after all. But surely he would want to turn the set off just to spite her? Another five minutes passed, and she had almost given up, when suddenly the cricket commentary stopped and there was only silence in the room. Turning, Maddy went quietly down the stairs with a big grin on her face.

Laura was home and came out of the sitting-room when she saw Maddy come down the stairs, her anxious frown changing to a look of surprise when she saw Maddy's face. 'What is it?'

'He's starting to fight,' Maddy said exultantly. 'I've made him so damn mad that he's started fighting just to get back at me.'

'Already? Oh, that's wonderful!'

Maddy's face sobered. 'Don't get too excited,' she warned. 'West's no fool and sooner or later he's going to see what I'm trying to do. Then he'll probably go back to doing nothing. But we'll just have to hope that by then he will want to go on fighting for his own sake.'

The two women had tea in the sitting-room and then Maddy said, 'If you don't mind, I think I'd like to take a walk round the garden.'

'Of course. You know you don't need to ask. I— I'd like you to feel that this is still your home. While— while you're here,' Laura finished awkwardly.

'Thank you.' Maddy gave a small smile. 'I'd like that—while I'm here.'

To cover the little embarrassment, Laura got quickly to her feet. 'And I'll go and sit with West.'

'Don't be surprised if he's angry with you,' Maddy cautioned. 'He'll blame you for bringing me here.'

'Don't worry,' Laura answered with a grim smile. 'If you can be tough, then so can I.'

'*No!* No, that wouldn't work,' Maddy added more slowly. 'All his hate must be directed at me. You must go on being sympathetic and kind. Just don't countermand anything that I've done, that's all.'

It had been nearly two years since Maddy had last seen High Beeches, but the garden hadn't changed very much. Possibly the flower beds weren't so neat and the plants wanted thinning, but the gardener still kept the lawns and hedges neat. She had always loved the garden and, as she slowly wandered round it, Maddy marvelled at the way shrubs and plants that she had planted with her own hands had grown and spread. The lawn sloped down to a wide rockery with steps in the middle of it leading down to a lower garden where there was a rose bed full of moss roses, a bed that West had put in for her as a first wedding anniversary present because he knew she loved them so. She had half expected that the roses would be gone, that West, in his anger and hurt pride, would have ripped them out. But the bushes were still there, although there were only a few faded blooms clinging to the branches and lifting their heads to the fading sun of the September afternoon. Going to one of the bushes, Maddy reached out to smell one of the roses, but the flower fell apart as she touched it, leaving a little pile of sweet-smelling silken petals in her hands. It's like our marriage, she thought fancifully: full and beautiful for a short time, and then falling apart and dying.

Suddenly she crushed the petals in her hand and threw them from her. That was the past, that was over. Getting West well was all that mattered now, and the sooner he was, the sooner she could go away and try to pick up that new life she'd started for herself.

Later Maddy helped Laura to prepare dinner, but refused to join her when she took a tray up to West's room. 'No, you eat with him. He's probably had enough of me for one day.' So she sat in the sitting-room watching the television, until Laura came down to let Sandy get West ready for the night.

'Was he very mad at you for bringing me here?'

'He was. But I told him the truth. I said that I'd tried nearly all the nursing agencies, but he'd been so nasty to the other nurses and physiotherapists that I'd hired that no one else wanted to come near him. Which left me no alternative but to approach you. I thought he'd ask me why you'd accepted,' she added in puzzlement, 'but he didn't. He seemed to have his own ideas about that.'

They went into the kitchen to do the washing up and were still there half an hour or so later when Sandy looked in to say goodnight. 'West's all settled down,' he told them.

'Already?' Maddy looked at the kitchen clock in surprise. 'But it's only nine-thirty.'

'Yes, but West doesn't sleep very well,' Laura explained. 'He's often awake most of the night. I often hear him stirring and see his light on.'

Maddy's gaze went from one to the other of them and she said decisively, 'Look, I think the three of us had better sit down and have a talk about this. Getting West back on his feet is going to be a battle, and battles are won much more easily if you have a properly prepared plan of campaign. Isn't that so, Sandy? You used to be a soldier.'

He gave a reluctant grin and nodded. 'Sounds like good sense to me.'

'Right. Let's start, then.' She pulled out a chair and sat at the kitchen table, the others joining her with slightly bemused looks on their faces. 'What I want to know first is where are Thor and Zeus?' she asked, naming West's two red setters.

'I've got them in a pen at the back of the garage block.'

'We didn't want them barking and disturbing West,' Laura added. 'Dogs can be so tiring when you're ill.'

'Yes, but he isn't ill, is he? Just incapacitated. And we've got to convince West of that, too,' Maddy said forcefully. 'Otherwise he's going to go on just lying there. We've got to show him that life is going to go on despite him, and that it's so good and interesting that he'd just better get down here and start joining in again.'

'Oh, Maddy, do you think we can?' Laura asked hopefully.

'We're going to have a darn good try. And for a start we'll have the dogs back. And you're going to stop tiptoeing around the house and not putting the radio on, Laura. You always used to listen to it and you're going to now—the louder the better. This place is much too quiet—we've got to liven it up. Don't worry if it annoys him or wakes him up; he's supposed to sleep at night, not during the day. Now, what about visitors?'

'He won't see anyone,' Laura answered, her eyes bleak again.

'No one? Not even his racing friends?'

Sandy shook his head. 'Quite a few of them went to the hospital to see him, but when West refused they stopped coming. It's natural enough; they lead busy lives and they're out of the country most of the summer.'

'Well, we must start encouraging visitors again. And don't ask him, just show them in. And the younger and more fit they are, the better. Let him know what he's missing.' She looked at her mother-in-law. 'And how about you, Laura? You used to entertain your friends here a lot. Do you still do that?'

'Oh, no, I didn't think it right to . . .' She broke off and nodded. 'Yes, I understand, I'll phone round and see if I can make up a bridge party for tomorrow night.'

'Good. And invite that ex-major who always laughs so loudly. I want West to hear what's going on.'

Laura laughed, her eyes sparkling, and to hear her laugh when she'd been so low was almost reward in itself.

Maddy looked at Sandy. 'How about those veteran-car enthusiast cronies of yours that go down to the local pub? West quite often used to go down there with you and have a drink with them, didn't he?'

'Yes, but he hasn't done, not since—well, not for quite a while before his accident.'

Maddy guessed that he'd been going to say since she'd left West, and she bit her lip a little but said firmly, 'In that case you'll have a lot to catch up on. Try and get them to come round here and have a drink with him one evening next week, will you?' Sandy nodded and she sat back. 'OK, so we'll do those things for a start. And if he starts getting annoyed, push all the blame on me.'

Laura gave her a steady look. 'But can you take it? It will require a great deal of strength—especially if you still care at all about him.'

Maddy stood up, her fingertips pressed against the varnished top of the pine table. 'Then I had better be extremely detached and—uncaring, hadn't I?'

There was a soft glow of light under West's door when Maddy went up to bed an hour or so later. She tapped and went in. West turned his head to look at her then gazed back at the ceiling. She checked the medication chart and would have taken his pulse, but he immediately thrust his arm under the bedclothes.

'Do you need anything?'

'No.'

'Have you taken a sleeping pill?'

'No.'

'Do you want one?'

'I've already said no,' he snapped.

'Suit yourself.' She pushed the plug of the electric buzzer back into its socket and moved the button where West could reach it easily. 'This is for emergencies only, OK? Not so that you can turn everyone in this house into a slave to your bloody-mindedness. And before you get any ideas about keeping me awake all night with it, just remember that you will wake Laura too. And she deserves better than that from you.'

He didn't answer, just glared at her out of those haggard eyes, and Maddy went through the dressing-room to her own room, leaving the doors ajar behind her.

She could have done with a sleeping pill herself. It felt so strange to be back here in the house where she and West had been so happy. And so appallingly, hopelessly wretched. But it was the happy memories that prevailed. Those first years when they had been so in love and so eager to demonstrate that love. Maddy's body grew hot as she recalled so many nights of passion. And not only in the house but sometimes out in the woods, too, with the moon silvering their bodies or the sun dappling them with its warmth.

Would West ever hold a woman in his arms again? she wondered. And carry her with him to the heights of dizzy excitement? Yes, perhaps, one day, if she could give him back the will to live. But it wouldn't be her. He hated her so much that he couldn't even bear to touch her. She might give him back his life, but it would be for some other woman's love. But that was all right. That was OK, so long as he was alive and happy.

Some instinct woke her and Maddy sat up in bed, listening. A glance at the illuminated dial of her clock told her it was almost two. Switching on the bedside lamp, she slipped out of bed, pulled a dressing-gown over her pyjamas and went on bare feet to the door of West's room. She had already looked in on him at midnight, but he had been asleep then. Now he was awake, lying on his back with his arms stretched rigidly over the covers, his fists closed tightly. His eyes were creased shut and his jaw clenched towards the ceiling as he swore over and over again, his words a jumble, but their vehement meaning clear as he cursed the fate that had crippled him.

Maddy stood in the doorway, wondering whether to go away again and leave him to his private hell, but decided that the violent anger could be better spent. 'Feeling sorry for yourself, West?' she enquired calmly.

He became instantly still. *'Get out.'*

'I told you you should have taken a sleeping pill.'

'And I told you to get out,' he snarled.

'Want turning over?'

'No!'

'Want to talk?'

'With you? No way,' he snapped derisively.

Maddy began to walk round the other side of the bed, and West's eyes followed her balefully. 'I thought you were going to have the house painted this year,' she said conversationally. 'It must be three or four years since it was last done. The paint's peeling and it's starting to look really shabby.'

'What I do with the house is none of your damn business.'

'Tut, tut,' she admonished. 'All this swearing.' She stopped by the side of the bed and looked down at him. 'And what good does it do? Do you really think that lying there cursing is going to make any difference?'

'It makes me feel better, damn you.' He broke off, realising that he had sworn at her again.

'No, it doesn't. Nothing makes you feel better, West, because you won't let anyone help you, because you just want to lie there and wallow in your own misery!'

'Why, you...' West reached out for her with his left hand but she moved back a little, out of the way.

'You're a coward,' she taunted him. 'All those years I thought you were the bravest man I knew, when all the time you were nothing but a yellow coward. The first time you get hurt and you...'

'Shut up!' Her words were abruptly broken off as West yelled at her, his face taut with fury, and flung his right arm over his body to lunge forward and grab her wrist. 'Christ, you cruel bitch! What the hell have I done to deserve you? You made my life a hell on earth once, but I'm not going to let you do it again. Do you hear me?'

His fingers dug into her wrist, hurting her even though he was so weak. Taking a deep, unsteady breath, Maddy said, 'But you can't stop me, can you? As you said, you're in my power. And I can do and say anything to you that I want.'

'Don't you be so darn sure.' Exerting all his strength, he began to pull her towards him, the muscles in his neck becoming rigid as she resisted him.

She let him go on until the sweat stood out on his brow, then said, 'Just what are you trying to prove, West? So, you've got hold of me. So what? So, you can hurt me a little.' She looked at him tauntingly. 'But I can hurt you a hell of a lot more.'

His eyes glowered at her in the lamplight and his lips drew back into a snarl. 'And if you do,' he threatened, 'I'll put these hands round your lovely throat and I'll squeeze the life out of you, you cruel, sadistic little . . .'

Maddy suddenly jerked her wrist free from his hold and straightened up, her breathing uneven. 'Resorting to physical violence,' she mocked. 'How unlike the civilised, self-possessed West Marriott we all know and love. Or at least some of us love.' She laughed jeeringly. 'You haven't got the courage to face up to it, have you? *You crashed your car, West.* For once you got careless, or the gods weren't on your side, and you crashed. That's all it was—a car crash. Not the end of the world.' He tried to grab her again, but she moved back out of his reach and laughed scornfully. 'And you're lucky, don't you know that? You're alive. And the car didn't catch fire and burn you. So you're lucky!' Her voice had risen as her own emotions gripped her, but somehow Maddy managed to control them. 'Remember that next time you start feeling sorry for yourself.'

'I'm going to make you pay for this,' West spat at her. 'I'm going to make you pay if it's the last thing I do.'

'It probably will be, the way you're going on,' she said tauntingly. But then she gave a breathless kind of laugh. 'But at least there's one way that you won't be able to annoy me again.'

His brows drew into a puzzled frown. 'What do you mean?'

'That neither Sandy nor I are going to have to get up in the night to turn you over any more. You've just done it yourself.'

West stared at her, his eyes widening, and she went quickly from the room.

CHAPTER THREE

As USUAL, the next morning, Sandy went up to West first to give him his breakfast and get him ready to face yet another day in bed. But Maddy had promised that there would be some changes, and she lost no time in carrying them out. At ten o'clock she went up to West's room, and took Sandy and Laura with her.

She gave West a brisk 'Good morning,' but then ignored him as she said to Sandy, 'This bed is too wide and too low. I need a single bed that we can rest on wooden blocks to make it higher. Either that or we must hire a proper hospital bed. That would be better, of course, but . . .'

'I've had enough of hospital beds,' West broke in. 'And this one does me fine.'

'There's a single bed in the small guest room,' Laura offered. 'Would that do?'

'Oh, yes, I remember. That will do very well. Can you find some blocks to put under it, Sandy?'

Overriding West's angry protests, for the next hour they were all very busy swapping over the beds, the hardest part being when they had to lift West out of the original bed and put him in a chair while they made the change-over. They got him to the edge of the bed and he cursed them roundly as Maddy and Sandy took his weight to carry him to a nearby chair. But then the curses were abruptly broken off. Maddy looked quickly at his face and saw it taut with the effort to conceal harrowing pain. She didn't say anything, holding back a warning to Sandy to be gentle as they lowered West into the chair and put his legs up on a stool. He leaned back, his face deathly pale and beads of sweat on his brow and upper lip, in too much pain to be able to hide it. Slowly he opened his eyes, his teeth clenched and his knuckles showing white as he gripped the arms of the chair.

Maddy turned quickly away, unable to bear it, and became very brisk again, her face almost as pale as West's.

She made a point of not looking at him again until the new bed was ready for him and they had to lift him into it. Going to his side, she put her arm round him, the other under his knees, waiting for Sandy to come to do the same on West's other side. West's face was averted, but suddenly she felt a tremor run through him and he caught his breath. For a moment she thought she had hurt him, but there was something about his sudden rigidity that made her realise that it was far from being pain he'd felt. Maddy's eyes widened, but before she could even begin to think about it, Sandy had come over and she had to concentrate on hurting West as little as possible as they got him into the new bed.

They were more adept this time, and soon had him propped up against the pillows, at a height where Maddy could comfortably give him physiotherapy, and where he could see through the windows down to the drive and the garden beyond. Her voice a little unsteady, Maddy said, 'I think we all deserve a coffee after that. No, it's all right, I'll go down and make it.'

She ran down to the kitchen, wanting to be alone as much as to give West a chance to recover. Had that been a tremor of awareness that she had felt run through his body? But why not? Just because he was crippled, it didn't mean that he had lost his sexual appetite. And it must be a long time now since he had had sex with a woman. Briefly Maddy wondered if he had had affairs with many women since they had split up; she hadn't read of his name being linked with anyone in the Press, but, knowing how virile West was, she had little doubt that there had been other women. Not that they seemed to have hung around after his accident, she thought cynically. But that he should feel awareness of *her*, after all this time and with all the hatred that he felt for her... Maddy found the idea deeply disturbing. From West's physical point of view it might be a good sign, but from hers, knowing that she had to stay here and treat him, it could only make things that much more emotional and difficult.

The percolator boiled and she took a tray of coffee up to West's room for the three of them, but had her own in the kitchen, then went across to the garage to find the dogs. They were running around in a large pen at the back and knew her immediately, greeting her with barks of welcome, their long, silken tails wagging rapturously. Maddy let them out and they raced around in mad excitement at being let loose before she called them to heel and took them for a walk, going round past the front of the house so that West could see them from the window.

There was a beech wood not far from the house, the leaves just starting to turn to the gold of autumn. A place where she and West had frequently taken the dogs for a walk in the past. And now the two animals ran into it with joy, poking their noses down rabbit-holes, barking at anything that moved, and generally recapturing their lost paradise. After half an hour, Maddy took them back to the house, wiped their paws and took them up with her to West's room where he was now alone.

'Who the hell let them up...?' His anger was lost under the dogs' excited yelps, and he had to put up his hands to protect his face as they tried to lick him to death.

Maddy left them to it as she went into the dressing-room to prepare her physio equipment, and when she wheeled the trolley into the bedroom a few minutes later she found West with a hand on each of the dogs' heads, gently stroking them, a soft look around his mouth that only hardened when he heard her and looked up.

'I suppose it was your idea to let them in here,' he said shortly.

'Yes, it was. They'd been shut away in a pen at the back of the garage for fear of disturbing you. But I didn't see why they should be made to suffer just because you insist on being treated as an invalid.'

West opened his mouth to make an angry retort, but then said, 'No, you're right, they shouldn't have been shut away like that. I didn't know.'

'Did you bother to ask?' Maddy deliberately tried to needle him.

'I had one or two other things on my mind,' he answered tightly.

'Like feeling sorry for yourself?'

His lips thinned. 'Like trying to come to terms with—what I've become.'

'You mean with what you've let yourself become. You're not a cripple, West. You're not even an invalid. You're a convalescent. And if you don't know what that means, I'll tell you. It means that you're recovering, getting better. But just how fast you recover is up to you. And to how much of a fight you're willing to put up.'

West gave a snort of derision. 'What is this—your number one pep talk? Didn't they tell you? I'm never going to be able to walk again. *Or drive.* That should please you.'

'Why? Why should it please me?'

He gave a bitter laugh. 'Because you always wanted me to give it up, of course.'

'Yes, I wanted you to give it up, not be *made* to. Especially not like this.'

He looked at her for a moment, his underlip thrust out broodingly, but, before he could say anything, Maddy called the dogs and took them out of the room.

'Now what?' he demanded warily when she came back.

She gestured towards the trolley. 'Time for some physio treatment.'

'No way. Not by you.'

'All right.' Calmly she walked into the dressing-room and came back with a large folder in her hands. 'You'd better have these instead, then.' And she upturned the folder, letting a heap of brightly coloured leaflets fall on to the coverlet.

'What are they?' West demanded in surprise.

'Look for yourself. They're details of different wheelchairs, lifts, bath and bed hoists, that kind of thing. Choose which ones you want and I'll send off for them for you.'

'I don't want these.' West swept his arm across them, sending most of them on to the floor.

'Don't be silly, of course you do. You've decided to stay a cripple, haven't you? Cripples have to have lifts and wheelchairs. They have hoists to get them in and out of bed and the bath. Most of their body is just a useless lump that has to be dragged around after them. And, as you're determined to stay a cripple, you're going to need all these things.'

West just stared at her silently, his eyes murderous, and Maddy let that sink in before she added scornfully, 'You're a big man, West. You're heavy. You surely can't expect Sandy and me or Laura to break our backs lifting you around for the rest of your life? Oh, you'll get lighter, of course, as your legs gradually waste away, but paraplegics are so well looked after that they often live a normal lifespan. Not,' she pointed out cruelly, 'that you'll be a paraplegic—just a voluntary cripple.'

'God, you must really hate me,' said West harshly. 'Tell me just what it was that I did to you that turned you into the sadistic little she-devil you've become. I'd really like to know.'

Maddy's face tightened, but she ignored the gibe. 'Well, which is it to be—the wheelchair or the physio treatment?'

She waited, holding her breath, knowing that everything depended on his answer.

'What's the use?' West demanded angrily. 'They've said I won't be able to walk.'

'That isn't what the surgeon told me. He said "possibly". Sportsmen—and women—with injuries as bad as yours have walked again. But then, *they* had guts and determination.'

His mouth twisting cynically, West said, 'And you think I haven't?'

'I don't think you have, no. But I know you had once. Too much so,' she added in such a low tone that he didn't hear it.

'Maybe they had something worth fighting for,' he muttered.

'Don't you?' she asked, her eyes on his face as she moved nearer.

His grey eyes lifted to her face and grew bleak. 'No,' he answered in one curt, cold syllable. Maddy bit her lip hard and looked away, realising that she'd lost, but then turned swiftly as West said, 'There's only one thing I'd want to get well for.'

Her heart skipped a beat as she remembered the tremor that had run through him when she'd held him. 'What's that?' she asked unsteadily.

His eyes held hers, a glint of triumphant mockery in them as he said clearly, 'So that I can get in a car and race again, of course. What else?'

'What else?' Maddy agreed lightly, realising that West could be just as cruel as he used to be, and trying to hide the hurt. 'Only you could want to get well so that you could go and try to kill yourself all over again.'

West laughed suddenly. 'Just like old times, isn't it?' He lay back and looked at her scornfully. 'All right. Get on with your damned treatment, then.'

'It has to be a hundred per cent,' Maddy warned. 'No cutting out the exercises I give you.'

West looked at her for a moment and then let his eyes run over her, mentally stripping her. 'My dear Maddy,' he said sardonically, 'have I ever done *any-thing* less than one hundred percent?'

Bright spots of colour came into Maddy's cheeks and she turned away, knowing that was one skirmish that she'd lost, even if she'd already won the greater battle. But she got her own back when she turned to him a few seconds later and said, 'All right, take your pyjamas off.'

West's eyebrows shot up. 'Oh, no, I don't. I . . .'

But Maddy advanced on him threateningly. 'If you don't take them off, I will.'

'Quite the Amazon,' he mocked, but his hand wasn't quite steady as he unbuttoned his pyjama jacket and pulled it off.

The deep tan he'd always had hadn't completely faded; his skin was still a pale gold and his chest as wide and muscular as ever. But then he had always kept himself very fit, spending at least an hour every day exercising in a small gym in the basement, so it would take quite a long time before his body began to waste. She put her hands gently on the arm that he had broken and tried to ignore its rigidity as tension gripped West's body.

As impersonally as she could, she bent the arm and straightened it again. 'Does it still give you any pain? The truth, please.'

He glanced at her searchingly, hesitated, but then said, 'Some. Not much.'

'OK. I'll start with that.'

She worked on his arm for a while, giving it deep heat and then ten minutes on the Interferaction machine to help his muscles to heal.

'I'll give you some exercises to do to help with that,' she remarked. 'But I'll do your legs first.' She went to pull down the covers, but West grabbed them.

'Send Sandy up to me first,' he ordered firmly.

'For God's sake, West, we were married for four years. Such modesty is . . .'

'Just get him,' West snarled in a tone that she knew wasn't to be denied.

So Maddy did as he asked, and afterwards found that the mechanic had helped West to change from pyjamas into a pair of red and white bathing trunks.

'Very dashing,' she commented derisively. 'Now, can we get on?'

Deliberately she set out to keep her mind detached as she examined his legs, trying to ignore all the scar tissue as she gently ran her hands over them, trying to be impersonal as West flinched away from her touch. 'I'm sorry if I'm hurting you.'

He didn't answer, and she glanced up at his averted profile, saw his lips tightly clenched, his jaw rigid. To give him time to recover, she turned on the heat lamp and took out the chart she'd made of his legs, showing the positions of all the breaks and the pins, although she didn't really need to study it again; all the breakages were indelibly printed on her mind.

'What's that?' West took the chart from her and looked at it silently for some time. Then he said,

'They're a mess, aren't they? As you said, useless lumps of flesh.'

'Only if you let them become so,' she answered unevenly.

His eyes rose to meet hers, sudden suspicion in their depths. 'Why did you really come here?'

Realising that she'd let her guard slip, Maddy laughed and said, 'Oh, don't credit me with any altruistic ideals. I came here because it happened to suit me. I had—personal reasons for wanting to leave London at the moment.'

'What reasons?'

'Mind your own damn business,' Maddy retorted.

He eyed her narrowly, but her face remained impassive and he turned away, obviously having drawn his own conclusions. Maddy would have given a lot to know what those were, but at least her rebuff seemed to have allayed his suspicions. She'd have to be careful, she realised, West had always been very shrewd and acute; it would never do to let him find out that she had come here out of... Out of what? she wondered. Duty? Pity? Sentiment? Perhaps a combination of all three. None of which would be acceptable to West. Nor would the fourth alternative, that came unbidden into her mind and was instantaneously pushed away. They were divorced and she'd started a new life; there was no room in it for an old love, however deep that love had once been.

Turning off the lamp, Maddy picked up a jar of cream and began to rub ointment into West's legs where she was going to place the Interferaction pads. His body jerked and she said, 'Sorry if it's cold. I'll put the pads in place and you must tell me when you feel the vibration.'

'How often do you intend to do this?' West asked curtly.

'Twice a day,' Maddy returned promptly. 'Muscles can deteriorate very rapidly if they're not used for any length of time.'

She spoke matter-of-factly, trying to dispel the tension that hovered in the air, a tension created by West's resentment at her working on his near-naked body, and her own remembrance of the dizzy heights of passion and pleasure that his body had taken her to. When he'd been whole and able to take her when he pleased. But now he could only lie here helplessly, and she knew that to West, who had taken a masculine pride in his strength and virility, it must be an added torment to have her see him like this.

When she'd finished the front of his legs she said, 'I have to do the backs now. Can you turn yourself over, or shall I help you?'

He gave her a look, but started to try and turn himself using only his arms. Maddy turned away and pretended to busy herself with some crêpe bandages, trying to close her ears to the bitten-off groan of pain, and hoping to God that he wouldn't fall out of the bed and injure himself further. But after what seemed like hours, he said gruffly, 'All right, damn you. I'm over.'

His body was still quivering with the effort it had cost him, a light dew of sweat on his skin that she had to carefully wipe off before she could apply the Interferaction pads. Maddy bit her lip, knowing the effort it must have cost him, and knowing, too, all the hard work it was going to take over the next weeks and months if he was ever to walk again. With his back to her and his face turned away, Maddy didn't have to hide the emotion in her face. She reached out and almost touched his blond hair, but then drew back, her eyes desolate, as she realised that she no longer had the right to touch him, and that hers was no longer the role of comforter.

It was almost lunch time before she'd finished, and she was still packing her equipment when Laura brought up a tray. She gave Maddy a quick look, her eyes bright with hope, although that died a little when she saw the exhaustion on West's face. But Maddy gave her a discreet wink and Laura rallied to say, 'You will join us for lunch, won't you, Maddy?'

West opened pain-racked eyes. 'Lowering yourself to eat with the hired help now, Mother?' he jeered tauntingly.

'West! Really!' There was genuine anger in Laura's voice. 'You will apologise to Maddy at once.'

Maddy laughed. 'Oh, don't make him do that; it'll set him back at least a week.' She came to stand by his bed and looked down at West mockingly. 'You don't have a choice where or when you eat, but I do. And I don't choose to eat with *you*.' And she turned and walked quickly from the room, head high.

The afternoon was spent in taking the dogs for another walk and working out a chart of exercises for West, aimed at gradually building up his muscles without overtaxing the healing process. This she took up with her when she went to his room to give him his second session of therapy.

He studied it while she worked on him, but tossed it aside with an irritable, 'It's probably a complete waste of time.'

'You promised a one-hundred-per-cent effort. Remember?' Adding tartly, 'You can start them this evening. It will give you something to keep you occupied.'

'I don't need to be occupied. I spend the evenings with Mother. Surely you know that.'

'Not tonight you won't. And Laura won't be joining you for dinner, either.'

'Why? Is she going out?'

'No.'

She deliberately didn't explain further until West, goaded, said, 'All right, so what's happening tonight?'

'Only that Laura's invited some friends round for a bridge party.'

'And whose idea was that? Yours, I suppose.'

'Yes, it was. You're not an invalid, West. There's no need for everyone to pussyfoot around as if you're likely to have a relapse at the slightest noise—even if you are selfish enough to demand absolute quiet.'

She moved to turn off the heat lamp, but he caught her wrist. 'So you think I'm selfish, do you?'

'My God, West, I lived with you for four years. I don't *think* you're selfish, I know darn well you are.'

'For your information, I told Laura to go ahead with her entertaining as soon as they brought me home.'

'But I bet you told her in such a way that she'd have felt terrible if she had. I know you, West, you can tell someone to do something and at the same time convince them that that's the last thing you want.'

He gave a scornful laugh and dropped her wrist. 'That sounds extremely clever.'

'It is. Very clever—and very cruel. But then, you can be very cruel if you're not getting everything your own way. I know that, too.'

He glared at her. 'Well, you must be glad to see me so suitably punished, then, mustn't you?'

'And *that*,' Maddy emphasised, 'isn't the kind of remark that exactly endears you to anyone.'

'Who the hell wants to be endeared to anyone?' he snapped back. 'I certainly don't. I tried it once and found that the whole thing's just a cruel farce. You're lulled into believing that you're going to find happiness, and all you get is a kick in the guts.'

Maddy gasped, as much with surprise that he'd come out and said it as with indignation. Bitterly she said, 'You always manage to twist everything, don't you? You're always on the attack. But what's the point of bringing it up now? I told you two years ago that I'd made a mistake and should never have married you. I was crazy to think that love could—that I could change you. And stupid to think that I was strong enough to withstand the fear every time you raced. So I left. I had a choice and I made it. Whereas it seemed that you had no choice. It wasn't me or racing—I didn't even come into it, did I?'

She was glaring at him, her breathing uneven, but turned abruptly away, angry with herself for having lost her temper. Or rather, having been goaded into losing it.

'So you're not completely impersonal, after all,' West said in malicious triumph.

'No,' she admitted. 'I'm angry that I wasted so much of my life.' She turned off the Interferaction and removed the pads from West's legs. 'That should do for today. Don't forget to do the exercises,' she instructed shortly. 'Sandy will bring a meal up for you later.'

West didn't answer. His eyes were fixed on her face, a frown between his brows. Quickly Maddy cleaned up and pushed the trolley back into the dressing-room, then washed her hands and automatically looked in on West to make sure he was comfortable before she went downstairs.

'Have you got everything you need?'

'Yes.' She turned to go, but he said, 'Maddy, wait. I want to talk to you.'

'Sorry, I promised to help Laura prepare supper.'

'Come up this evening, then.'

Maddy gave him a surprised glance, wondering what he wanted. The frown was still between his eyes and his mouth was set in a grim line. It didn't take more than a second to decide that she didn't want to talk to him when he was in that kind of mood. One row like today's was as much as she could take. 'Sorry,' she said again. 'I'm the hired help. Remember? And tonight happens to be my night off. So you'll just have to put up with your own company.'

Immediately after dinner, Maddy drove into the nearest town to see a film, having left instructions with Sandy to make sure West did his exercises. She didn't really enjoy the film, although it was quite a good comedy; she just didn't like being there on her own. That had been one of the hardest things to get used to, knowing that she was alone. Even when West had been away and she had gone somewhere by herself it had been different: there had always been the inner knowledge that she was a part of something, that her life was shared, not only now but in the future. But now the future was something she had learned not to think about; when you were on your own it was much easier to live from day to day.

The bridge party was still going on when she got back to the house, and she went into the kitchen to clear the supper things, deliberately not going up to see how West was. She didn't even go in to see him when she went up to bed, leaving it until about two in the morning before she crept quietly into his room from her own. He was deeply asleep, the physical effort of the treatment and exercise having tired him out. His face was more relaxed, the lines of bitterness and pain around his mouth softened in sleep. Maddy stood looking down at him, remembering their honeymoon, when she had often woken in the night to watch West while he slept, marvelling at the miracle of being his wife, of being in his bed, of knowing that he loved her. Sometimes he hadn't woken when she had snuggled up against him and she had gone back to sleep, but other times he had, and then he would reach for her and neither of them would sleep until they lay exhausted again in each other's arms. Together. Close. A never-to-be-broken unity.

Tenderly Maddy reached out and touched West's hair, smoothing it with her fingers. He muttered in his sleep and moved restlessly, almost as if he was shaking off her hand. Quickly she withdrew it and went back to her own room.

During the next few days Maddy established a routine of therapy and exercises for West, giving him two hours both morning and afternoon. At first the exercises tired him considerably, but there was no way he was going to admit to it. He worked at them grimly to the end, then lay back on pillows, ashen-faced, but with malicious triumph in his eyes. His determination was fed by anger, and Maddy was careful to keep it fuelled. She mocked him when she knew that he'd thought he'd done well with the exercises, annoyed him by using his study again, and aroused his frustration in a dozen different ways: by turning on his television, playing records too loudly, and letting the dogs bark under his window.

But West in turn knew her weakness and retaliated unmercifully. When she went into his room one afternoon she found him watching a video of a Grand Prix race. It was a race that he'd won a couple of years ago, just before she'd left him. Maddy remembered it vividly because it was one of the factors that had made her leave. The conditions were terrible, the cars trying to speed round the circuit in pouring, almost torrential rain, and there had been more than one collision that day. West himself had spun off at one point, but had managed to get back on the track to win the race. Maddy had watched it on television and immediately afterwards begged West yet again to retire, but, flushed with his success, he had only laughed and told her not to be such a cowardly idiot.

So now he put it on, knowing that it would get to her. Maddy tried to ignore it, but West deliberately turned the sound up high and the commentator's voice bit into her brain. West eyed her malevolently as she switched on the heat lamp and busied herself with the trolley, trying to shut out the roar of the engines, the nightmare noise that even now sometimes brought her awake in the night, sweating with fear. The commentator's voice rose and she knew they were coming to the part of the race where West spun off. Her chest tightening unbearably, Maddy suddenly reached out to grab the remote control from where it lay on his lap and turn it off. But West was too quick for her and reached it first, holding it out of her reach.

'What's the matter?' he taunted. 'Can't you take it?'

Maddy straightened up, her face taut. 'You're a sadistic swine, West.'

'Yeah? You don't do so badly in that area, either.'

They glared at each other for a moment, but then West pressed the stop button and the grating roar of the engines suddenly ceased. He made a petulant movement with his hand. 'Why the hell did you marry me if you hated racing so much?' he demanded forcefully.

Maddy reached up to adjust the lamp, her hand not quite steady. 'I hardly think there's any point in discussing that now. It's over, and I . . .'

'Tell me,' West insisted harshly.

She looked down at his hawklike face, still so heart-catchingly thin, and turned away, walking over to the window. 'I didn't hate racing at first. You know that. I found it as exciting as you did. But after we were married I began to be afraid for you. And the fear just—just grew, until I couldn't take it any more.' She gave a short laugh and looked down at her hands. 'Stupid, I know, to be afraid for you when you had absolutely no fear for yourself. But there it is. Women—women sometimes get like that.' She turned to face him, the sun from the window shining through her hair, framing her in the golden rays. 'But you knew I was afraid. You knew that every race tore me apart. But you only got angry. My fears—embarrassed you. You became ashamed of me.'

West had been listening to her keenly, but now he turned away. 'I couldn't understand why you'd changed. I still can't.'

'Can't you? It's really very simple.' Maddy came over and moved the lamp, directing it on his legs, fully in control of herself again now.

'So tell me.'

She gave a small laugh. 'Oh, no, it's much too late for that. The fact that you couldn't understand why I felt that way was one of the reasons why I left you. But if you couldn't understand then, I'm sure you can't now.'

He gave her a baffled look then caught hold of her hand when she went to move away. She tried to pull free but he held her firmly, frowning angrily down at her hand. 'Why did you send your rings back to me after the divorce?'

'Because I wasn't your wife any more,' she answered as steadily as she could. 'I had no right to wear them.'

'That's rubbish. They were yours. They weren't given with the proviso that if we broke up I'd want them back.'

'I know that, but . . .'

His fingers tightened on hers. 'I suppose you looked on them as one of the shackles of an unhappy marriage and couldn't wait to get rid of them,' he said harshly. 'Although you seemed happy enough when I gave them to you.' Maddy was silent as he cast her hand aside contemptuously. 'You should have sold them—or thrown them away.'

'I'm sorry if I hurt you by sending them back, but I . . .'

'Damn it, you didn't hurt me. Nothing you can do can hurt me!' But the violent tone in which he said it utterly belied his words.

After that, West was deliberately cold and distant with her, resisting even her best efforts to annoy him and looking at her sardonically when she did so, so that Maddy began to be afraid that his anger might fade and not be enough to drive him on. She realised that she would have to think of something else that would compel him to carry on with the exercises for their own sake, because he was really only doing them now to spite her, with no real conviction that he would ever walk again.

The opportunity came a couple of weeks after she'd arrived at High Beeches, but at first she didn't even realise it. Maddy was walking back to the house after taking the dogs for a walk late one morning and found a man standing on the doorstep. The dogs barked and he turned, his eyes widening a little when he saw Maddy hurrying towards him, her hair windswept and a flush of colour in her cheeks from running with the dogs.

'Good morning,' she called out as she came up. 'Can I help you?'

'I hope so. I called to see Mr Marriott, but there doesn't seem to be anyone around. Perhaps I should have phoned first.'

'Perhaps it would have been better. Everyone's out at the moment.' Maddy looked at him curiously. He was young, about the same age as West, with dark hair and pleasant good looks, but she didn't recognise him as one of West's friends. 'Is West expecting you? He didn't mention that a guest was coming today.'

The man grinned. 'I'm afraid I can hardly be called a guest. I'm Mr Marriott's doctor.'

'Oh!' Her eyebrows rose in surprise. 'But his doctor is...' Then she realised and said, 'Oh, you mean you're the local doctor. But surely that's Doctor Mackintosh?'

'It was, but he retired last year and I took over the practice.' He held out his hand to her. 'I'm Doctor Roberts. Tim Roberts.'

'Hello.' Maddy shook his hand, her own held in a firm grip. 'I'm West's—West's nurse. Madeline French.'

'Ah, another new one. How long have you been here?'

Maddy grinned. 'Nearly two weeks.' She opened the door and motioned him in.

'And he hasn't managed to get rid of you yet? You must be tougher than you look.'

'Oh, I am.' She paused in the hall to take off her jacket and preceded him up the stairs, unaware of the admiring look he gave her slim figure in a loose sweater, and jeans tucked into knee-high boots.

West was reading when they went into his room, but his head came up quickly as Maddy laughed at something the doctor said to her. His eyes narrowed, but he made no comment other than to greet Dr Roberts.

'You're looking better,' the latter observed, taking his pulse. 'It must be having such an attractive nurse.' And he smiled across at Maddy, who was leaning against the window sill.

West shot him a look. 'You've met my . . .'

'Nurse French, yes. We introduced ourselves on the doorstep.'

'How often do you call?' Maddy asked, amusement in her voice at the sardonic look West shot at her.

'At least once a week. I must have missed you when I called last week. Perhaps it was your day off.'

'Oh, I don't have a specific day. I just take time when I can.'

Dr Roberts had thrust a thermometer into West's mouth, much to his indignation. 'Well, your patient seems to be doing well in your care. What treatment are you giving him?'

Maddy told him, inwardly laughing at the growing anger in West's eyes at being ignored.

When the thermometer was at last removed he said sarcastically, 'It would have been the same with any nurse.'

'I hardly think so. You're lucky to have someone like Nurse French, who can combine physiotherapy with nursing.'

'Oh, yes,' West agreed caustically. 'Extremely lucky.'

Tim Roberts' eyebrows rose in surprise at his tone, but he looked at Maddy, his glance frankly admiring, and said, 'Yes, you are.'

Maddy noted the warmth in his eyes and voice, and would have dismissed it if she hadn't seen the effect it had on West. His face hardened and his hand clenched on the coverlet. My God, she thought, he's jealous. He's actually jealous. And suddenly she knew that she had a new weapon in the fight to get West walking again. So she smiled back at Tim Roberts, put her hands behind her on the window sill to better show off her figure and said, 'Why, thank you. And I'm usually called Maddy.'

'Maddy it is, then.' His eyes lingered on her for a moment, but then he remembered why he was there. 'How are the medical supplies going?'

He crossed to the medicine table and Maddy went to join him, standing quite close as he wrote out a prescription for further supplies. 'Well, I think that's everything,' he said reluctantly. 'Glad to see you looking so much better, Marriott.'

'And thank you so much for calling,' West returned acidly.

But his sarcasm was lost on Tim as Maddy said, 'I'll show you out,' and he followed her downstairs.

In the hall he turned to her. 'How about your evenings, are they free?' She hesitated for a moment, wondering whether she ought to let things go further, but he mistook her hesitation and said, 'I'm sorry, you probably think I'm rushing you, but I would like to see you again, Maddy. Before you get fed up with Marriott and disappear. So—will you have dinner with me one evening?'

'That would be very nice, but I . . .' Again she hesitated, wondering whether she ought to accept.

'I'm not married or anything,' he assured her. 'And I'm fit and healthy and terribly respectable. Also, I promise not to talk shop all evening.'

Maddy gave a gurgle of laughter. 'With such a recommendation, how can a girl refuse? All right, I'd like to.'

'Good.' he gave her a warm smile. 'How about Saturday? I'll pick you up at seven?'

'That will be fine. See you Saturday, then.'

After closing the door behind him, Maddy leant on it for a moment, wondering if she was doing the right thing. But if it did make West jealous and that spurred him on...

She ran lightly back up the stairs and found West watching Tim drive away through the window. 'Quite some conference you had downstairs,' he remarked sarcastically. 'And were you discussing my progress, by any remote chance?'

'Why, no.' Maddy too went to look out of the window, and said with deliberate uninterestedness, 'As a matter of fact, we didn't mention you at all.' She turned to where a full-length mirror fronted a wardrobe door and looked at her reflection, lifting her hair back off her face and tilting her head to see the effect.

Behind her she saw a look of torment come into West's face as he clamped his teeth shut, his jaw rigid, and she knew that this ploy, too, was going to work.

CHAPTER FOUR

MADDY swung round from the mirror, her eyes bright. 'I'm fixing lunch today; what would you like?'

But West was apparently uninterested in food. His grey eyes were on her face, studying her almost as if she were a stranger. As if he was trying to see her as Tim Roberts had: a young, vital, and good-looking girl who was still very sexually attractive to men. West's eyes moved down her slim figure, possibly remembering the first time he had ever seen her himself, when he had given a friend a lift to a physiotherapy clinic where Maddy had just started work after finishing her training. Maybe what they felt for each other wasn't love at first sight, but it had certainly been instant physical attraction. An attraction that had soon become overpowering and had grown into love, a love that for Maddy had gone on growing even after the first fierce physical desire had been satiated.

But had it for West? She knew that he had loved her, but had come to believe that it wasn't the overwhelming love she felt for him. If it had been, he would have done as she'd begged and given up racing. But the physical attraction had never died, and their lovemaking had always been wildly exciting—until West had begun to use it as a weapon, a means to overcome her when they rowed, or to quieten and distract her when she tried to put her case calmly and rationally.

And it seemed that even now the attraction was still there, for West at least, his eyes darkening as they ran over her and his tongue licking lips suddenly gone dry. 'Why didn't you tell him who you were?' he demanded thickly.

'I did. I told him I was your nurse.'

'Don't be obtuse. You know exactly what I mean.'

'All right.' She shrugged. 'What would be the point? We're no longer married, so why claim the relationship? After all, we mean nothing to each other now.' She watched him under her lashes, studying his face to see his reaction, and wasn't disappointed.

West's brows drew into a frown and he said, 'Do you always use your maiden name now, or is that just because you're here?'

'No, I always use it.'

His eyes met hers in scarcely controlled anger. 'You still have the right to use mine,' he pointed out abruptly. 'It's still legally your name.'

Maddy shook her head. 'I don't agree. I'm no longer your wife, so I don't see that I have either the right or the need to use your name. Our—ties have been broken. We're leading completely separate lives again. It's—it's almost as if the marriage had never happened, so I . . .'

West's jeering laugh broke in on her. 'Is that what you're trying to do, pretend it never happened? My God, if you can deceive yourself into thinking that . . .'

'No. No, I'm not trying to do that.' Maddy thrust her hands into her pockets, safely hidden beneath her sweater. 'But sometimes that life seems so unreal now. Almost like a dream.' Her eyes lifted to his. 'Or a nightmare.'

His lips thinned. 'Oh, I quite agree there. But you can't shut it out,' he added brusquely. 'The memory of it, the fact that it failed, is always there.'

Maddy's eyes widened. 'Even now? After all this time that we've been apart?'

'Failure isn't a thing I'm likely to forget,' he pointed out shortly. 'And it isn't so long; we've been divorced less than a year.'

'No, I suppose not.'

They were both silent for a long moment until West said harshly, 'Has he asked you out—Tim Roberts?'

For a moment she was on the point of telling him it was none of his business, but then Maddy changed her mind and nodded. 'Yes, he has.'

'He certainly doesn't waste any time,' West remarked with a snort of derision.

'That's your fault,' Maddy told him with a grin. 'He's afraid I won't be able to stand nursing you for much longer and I'll leave like all the others. Which reminds me,' she crossed to stand beside his bed, 'I've won our bet; I've stayed here longer than all the others did.'

'So you have. You've clung like the veritable limpet,' West observed scathingly. 'And now I suppose you want to claim the prize—whatever it's to be.'

'Mm, but I haven't made up my mind what I want yet. I'll have to think about it, and when I've decided on something—suitable, I'll let you know.'

She said it with mockery in her tone and West glared up at her. 'You think you're so damn clever, don't you? But the only reason you've stayed is because it does your ego good to think you have me in your power. But one day I'm going to turn the tables on you and you won't be able to get out of here fast enough.'

Maddy laughed. 'I very much doubt that. So long as you're stuck in that bed there isn't a damn thing you can do about it.'

'Don't you be so sure,' West threatened grimly.

Maddy laughed again and made for the door, but just before she reached it, West called out sharply. 'Well, did you accept?'

'Accept?' Maddy turned, pretending not to know what he meant. West just glared at her in tight-lipped anger, and after hanging it out a few minutes longer she said, 'Oh, you mean Tim Roberts. Well—not that it's any concern of yours—but, yes, I accepted. I'm going out to dinner with him on Saturday.'

After that, things between them were strained to say the least. West deliberately set out to goad her beyond endurance; reminding her whenever he did his exercises that he was only doing it to get back to racing, demanding that she go out and buy him all the latest car-racing magazines, banging on the floor with an old cricket bat when she used his study, until she took it away from him, calling her on the internal telephone every ten minutes, and generally driving her to exasperation.

Maddy stood it all as patiently as she could, but wondered why he hadn't gone to these extremes when she'd first arrived—could it be that he hadn't been altogether sorry that she'd come?

As Saturday drew nearer things got worse, especially as he began to call out to her in the night and demand that she pick up a pillow or get him a drink. On the Friday Sandy and all the local veteran car enthusiasts spent the evening with him, which gave her a break, but after the men had gone and Sandy had settled him down for the night, he again called out to her.

'What is it now?' Maddy demanded tiredly. She had gone to bed to get an early night and was wearing a robe over her nightdress.

West looked her over, a glint of satisfaction in his eyes when he saw her stifle a yawn. 'I want something to read,' he said irritably.

'Laura got half a dozen books from the library for you only yesterday.'

But it was a mistake to argue with West when he was in this mood; he always had an answer to everything. 'Two of them I've read before, and I don't fancy the others. They're too heavy, I want something light.'

'So read a magazine or something, then.' Honestly, it was like arguing with a child.

'I've read everything in sight,' he said petulantly. 'Go and get me a P.G. Wodehouse from my study.'

'Which one?'

'Any one. Use your common sense.'

Maddy gave him a fulminating look, but did as he asked, cautiously coming back with four books in case he complained. 'There. And if you call out again I shan't come.'

'What if I get ill suddenly, or fall out of bed?'

'Then you'll just have to stay there,' she answered brutally, and meant it. 'I'm going to bed.'

'No, stay. Stay and talk for a while.' His voice changed as he looked at her broodingly. 'Tell me about

your life since we broke up. Have you been doing this
sort of thing ever since you walked out on me?'

Maddy could have argued with that last assertion,
but let it pass. 'Nursing? Yes.'

'And do you find it—satisfying?'

'I don't think that's exactly how I would describe
it. It's my profession, the way I earn my living. Sometimes it can be quite harrowing, but . . .'

'How do you mean?'

She shrugged eloquently. 'Sometimes your patients
don't get well. And there comes a time when they re-
alize it themselves.' She paused, her mind looking
inward into the past. 'Then it becomes very—hard.'

West frowned, then said, 'But at other times?'

'As I said, it's my job. you get some patients who
are really nice, and others,' she looked at West mean-
ingfully, 'who are extremely difficult.'

His lips curled sardonically. 'And I suppose you
class me as one of the difficult ones.'

'Oh, no,' she returned sweetly, 'not difficult—more
downright bloody-minded.'

He shot her a look out of eyes that narrowed balefully. 'And are your patients mixed—or are they all
men?'

'No, I look after whichever patients the agency
thinks I'm best qualified to nurse.'

'But I bet you have better results with the men.'

Maddy stiffened. 'What's that supposed to mean?'

'Oh, I think you know exactly what I mean.' Suddenly West lunged out and caught her arm, jerking
her forward so that she lost her footing and stumbled
against the bed, half lying on it. His breathing harsh,
West's fingers bit into her flesh, holding her so that

she was unable to get away. 'Yes,' he repeated, 'you
know what I mean. The same reason you don't wear
a uniform, or even an overall like the other nurses.
Because you try and turn your patients on, don't you?
Flaunting yourself in those figure-hugging jeans and
with your hair loose. Or if it's not the patient, then
it's probably the patient's husband.' His grip tightened
unmercifully. 'Tell me, just how much therapy do you
give the husbands when your patients are tucked up
in bed at night and safely doped with sleeping pills
to keep them quiet?'

Maddy's face whitened, but, off balance as she was,
she couldn't break free of West's iron grip, and he
laughed when she struggled to do so.

'That therapy treatment you've been giving me has
worked too well—I'm stronger that you again now.'

'West, this is stupid. What do you think you're
trying to prove? Let go of me, I want to go back to
bed.'

'To an empty bed?' he mocked. 'Surely not.' He
put his free hand under her chin, making her look at
him. 'You always were a sexy little cat. It's what I
first noticed about you. And I was proved more than
right—after I'd given you a few lessons.'

'Damn it, West, you're hurting me. Let go.'

'When I'm good and ready.' His grey eyes were
intent on her face, going over each feature as if reminding himself of how she had looked when he had
first discovered her unawakened sensuality. 'Yes,' he
went on softly, 'you soon turned into a very hot little
number in bed. Once you'd found out what it was
like you couldn't get enough, could you?'

'*Stop it!* I don't have to take this from ...'

But he jerked her head up, cutting off her words. 'And what about now?' he demanded, his voice becoming suddenly harsh. 'Who do you get to satisfy you since you left me? Do you have another man— or men? Well, do you?'

'How dare you? How dare you speak to me like that?' Maddy tried to knock his hand away and stand, but he still held her.

'Tell me,' he ordered fiercely. 'I want to know.'

'Why? So you can throw it back at me?'

'So there have been others!' he pounced.

His fingers hurt her and suddenly Maddy was frightened. West had always been as jealous as hell where anything he took pride in possessing was concerned. Like her—or his favourite car. The thought steadied her and she took a long breath, realising that she had stirred up deeper emotions that she'd realised when she'd set out to make West jealous. Coldly she said, 'You have no right to question me like this. My life is my own now. Whether I go out with other men or not is none of your damn business.' She looked steadily into his eyes. 'I'm free, West. I don't belong to you any more. I'm just as free to choose as you are.'

His lips curled moodily. 'You're far too young and attractive for there not to have been others.'

Maddy gave a rather unsteady laugh. 'Well, thanks for the compliment.'

As if he immediately regretted it, West added disparagingly, 'Especially if you thrust yourself at them as you did Tim Roberts.'

More in command of herself now, Maddy said, 'It's no good trying to provoke me, West. I'm not going to quarrel with you and I'm not going to tell you anything about my private life.'

' "Your private life",' he repeated scornfully. 'You sound like a coy actress.' But then his mood changed suddenly and he said in a bleak voice, 'Once you were *my* private life. The woman I went home to, for solace—and love. My very private woman that I thought would always be there, waiting for me.' His face had softened for a moment, but almost instantly it hardened again. 'But now what are you—any available man's for the taking?'

Maddy made an indignant sound, but any words were silenced by the bleak bitterness in his voice.

His hand tightening on her arm, West began to pull her down towards him. His angular face was sharpened by tension and there was a cold glitter in his eyes as they held hers. 'But can they make you feel like I did?' he said in a fierce whisper. 'Do they make you beg for more? Do they make you cry because it was so good?' Lifting his other hand, he put it behind her head and forced her down towards him.

'No, West. No. *Please.*'

She tried to resist, her neck muscles rigid, but West was far too strong for her, and he continued to compel her towards him until her furious face was only a couple of inches from his own. He laughed softly, enjoying his physical power over her, but then his eyes darkened and he kissed her.

At first Maddy's only emotion was rage, and she struggled against him, twisting and jerking her head in an effort to break free. But West simply put his hand in her hair and laughed against her mouth as he went on kissing her. She tried to bite him and he swore, tasting blood on his lip. His hands tightened and he jerked her forward across the bed so that she was lying across his lap, her face under his now and at the mercy of his fierce anger as his bruising lips forced her to open her mouth and let him in.

Furiously she beat against his chest, forgetting all about his injuries, and made inarticulate sounds of protest that slowly died as awareness stealthily grew and hunger took the place of anger. So intent was he on subduing her that for a moment West didn't re-alise that she'd stopped fighting him. But then his breath caught in his throat and he kissed her avidly, with the compulsion of a man who had too long been denied.

Maddy gave a little whimper under her breath and her arms went round his neck. It was like coming home after being away for a long, long time. It felt so right. So right. Her heart filled with happiness, grew so full that it hurt, and her body began to flame as she drowned in his kiss, lost to everything as she was swept into a molten sea of desire and passion.

When West at last lifted his head, she lay trembling beneath him, eyes closed, her mouth soft and yielding. He looked down at her for a moment, then lifted his hand to undo her gown and push aside the thin ma-terial of her nightdress until he found her breast. A great tremor ran through her as he touched her, and Maddy opened heavy-lidded eyes to look into his. There was sensuousness in their deep blue depths and a dawning hope that shone beneath her thick lashes. But as she looked up into West's face and she saw the derisive triumph there, sensuousness and hope quickly died, to be replaced by the chill realisation that he had deliberately set out to humiliate her.

Immediately she tried to get up, but West held her down, his hand still on her breast, caressing her skilfully as he said in soft mockery, 'See how right I was. You're just as hungry for sex as ever. And do your new lovers make you feel the way I did? Do they?' he demanded, his face sharpening.

Strangely, Maddy didn't feel angry any more, only terribly sad, the sadness reaching right into her soul. 'The game's over, West. Let me up.'

His eyes widened a little in surprise at her flat tone, and he caressed her again. trying to arouse her, but when he saw that it was useless, West sat back abruptly and released her. Awkwardly, Maddy pushed herself to her feet and turned to face him, tying her robe with hands that weren't quite steady. 'Thank you,' she said tightly.

West's eyebrows rose. 'Thank you? For what?'

'For reminding me of just why I left you.'

His jaw hardened, but before West could speak Maddy had turned and walked out of the room, firmly closing the door behind her.

On the Saturday morning and afternoon Maddy gave West his treatment as usual, but neither of them was in a mood to talk. West looked at her broodingly under frowning brows, but Maddy was coldly impersonal, just a professional who was doing a job and nothing more. The impetus to make West jealous was well and truly dead, and she regretted even starting it. That West could still be so possessive after all this time, and so vindictive in his jealousy, had shaken her badly, and she had no wish to repeat the experience.

If it hadn't meant that it would be a further victory for West, she would have broken her date with Tim Roberts. She certainly didn't feel like going out; she had hardly slept after that nasty scene with West, her mind going over it again and again and wishing to God that she hadn't succumbed to his kiss. But it had brought so many memories back, and her yearning body had betrayed her.

Well, she would just have to make sure that she didn't yield to weakness ever again, Maddy resolved. And she must always be on her guard against West, because now that he had found out that she wasn't immune to him he would use it against her. That, at least, she *was* sure of.

Because of her sleepless night, Maddy took a nap in the late afternoon, but slept longer than she'd intended and had to rush to get ready, a thing she hated. She'd had to tell Laura that she was going out to dinner with Tim Roberts, and at first the older woman had frowned disapprovingly, but when Maddy explained that it was only to try and annoy West, Laura had laughed delightedly. Now she welcomed him in and was her usual charming self as they waited for Maddy to come downstairs, Laura having gone into the hall and called up that he was there, loud enough for West to hear.

Maddy hurried down a few minutes later and Tim's eyes went over her admiringly as he rose to greet her. She had put on one of the designer dresses left over from her marriage, and wore her hair in a thick braid threaded with a matching ribbon, a style that was both sophisticated and charming, and she didn't have to look in the mirror to know that she looked good. She greeted Tim quite naturally, shaking his hand before accepting a drink from Laura. They chatted together for a little while, but then the first of Laura's bridge party guests arrived, and Tim and Maddy left to drive to a restaurant in a nearby town.

'This is new, isn't it?' Maddy remarked as they walked up to the attractively lit doorway. 'I seem to remember the place as being a rather run-down wine bar.'

'Yes, that's right. The wine bar went out of business about four months ago.' Tim helped her off with her coat and they sat in the little bar. 'Do you know the area, then?'

'Er—yes. I lived quite near here for a while.'

Tim looked as if he was going to ask her more, but fortunately a waiter came up with menus and took their order for drinks.

'How do you like it here?' Maddy asked quickly before Tim could get his question in.

'Very much. It took a little getting used to at first, because I used to be in a practice in Birmingham. But I much prefer being in the country.'

'Did you train in Birmingham?'

For a while Tim talked about himself, making Maddy laugh about some of the things that had happened to him while he was a medical school, but when they'd ordered and were sitting at their table in the restaurant, he said, 'How about you? Combining physiotherapy and nursing is rather unusual, isn't it?'

'I suppose it is a little. But I trained as a physio first and then found I had some time on my hands and decided to take up nursing. And of course, all the studying I'd had to do on anatomy and that kind of thing was a great help with the nursing.'

'It must have been. But why bother to take up a second profession when you already had a perfectly good one?'

Maddy hesitated. 'I—needed a challenge, I suppose,' she said slowly, remembering how empty her life had become when West was away, often for months on end.

'Well, you must be reaping all the advantages of it now. I imagine it must be pretty lucrative looking after specialist cases like West Marriott. What do you think of him, by the way?'

'Hey,' Maddy remonstrated. 'You promised not to talk shop.'

Tim laughed. 'No, not as a patient, as a man.'

'Oh. As a man.' She hesitated, feeling both the best and the least qualified to answer that. 'What do you?' she countered, cowardice getting the better of her.

'Well, I've only really got to know him since his accident, of course. Although I did treat him for a dose of 'flu not long after I came here. He was such a vital man, then. Full of energy. Terribly impatient to get better so he could rush off to take part in some race or other. But I didn't really get to know him very well then, because he was so withdrawn, of course.'

Maddy's eyes went swiftly to his. 'Withdrawn?'

'Yes. It was around the time his divorce came through, and it had hit him very hard. I think it was that that made him so restless; turning to work as a panacea, I suppose. Did you know his wife?'

Again she hesitated, realising that now was the time to tell Tim the truth, but she left it so long that he took her silence as a negative and went on with a note of anger in his voice, 'It seems she never once went to visit him in hospital, or since he's been home. She must be a heartless little bitch.'

'Maybe she—couldn't go and see him,' Maddy said hollowly.

'You mean she'd gone to live abroad or something? But West's crash was nearly six months ago; wherever she was she could have got on a boat or a plane and got back here by now. No, I reckon she just couldn't care less about him,' he stated shortly.

Maddy put down her fork, knowing it was too late to tell him now, but unable to look him in the face. 'Perhaps West didn't want his wife—his *ex*-wife to visit him.'

'That isn't what I heard when I went through his case notes with the sister at the hospital when I went to escort him home. She said that when West was first brought in, even when he was delirious from the anaesthetic, he was continuously calling for his wife.'

Maddy's eyes were fixed studiously on her plate as she took a very long time over buttering a piece of roll. 'But when he came round, surely he...'

'He went on asking for her, but after a week or so, of course, he realised that she wasn't going to show and he stopped asking. The sister said that after that he never once mentioned her name again. How can a woman be like that?' Tim added scornfully. 'After all, she'd lived with West, and she must have loved him once. But to just walk out on him and then to desert him when he needed her...'

'You don't know the circumstances,' Maddy broke in sharply. 'You have no right to judge.' Her voice hardened. 'And they were divorced; what right had West to ask for her when they were no longer married?'

'Because he still loved her, presumably. Although I doubt very much if he feels anything for her now—unless it's hatred, of course.'

'Do we have to talk about West Marriott?' Maddy demanded petulantly. 'I came out to get away from work.'

Tim was immediately contrite. 'Sorry. It's just that he's such an interesting person, and so famous. As a matter of fact I'm interested in car-racing myself.'

Oh, no! Maddy groaned inwardly. 'And do you actually race?' she asked in dread.

'Good heavens, no. I've neither the time, the money, nor the skill. The occasional round of golf is all I ever manage in the sporting line, I'm afraid.'

'But that sounds great. Very safe and very steady. Nice.'

Tim laughed. 'And very dull, I'm sure, after someone with as glamorous a career as West's.'

'I wouldn't call racing glamorous,' Maddy answered coldly. 'I'd call it—lethal.'

Abruptly she changed the subject and they talked about common interests: music, books, a love of the countryside that they both wished they had more time to indulge. 'At the moment,' Tim went on, 'I've got involved with the local drama group. Although I only help with making the sets and that sort of thing.'

'You have no ambitions to act?'

'It wouldn't be any good if I had. Supposing I was in the middle of some terribly gripping scene and I was called to an emergency.'

Maddy laughed, at ease again now. 'Yes, I see what you mean.'

'But they're always on the look-out for new talent. Why don't you give it a try? I'm sure with your looks you'd be an instant success.'

'But you don't know whether I can act,' she teased him. 'And I'm just as tied as you are.'

'Oh, but surely you can arrange to have nights off to attend rehearsals? They'll be casting for a new play in a week or so; if you like I could take you down and introduce you to everyone and you could...'

Maddy shook her head dismissively. 'You forget, I'm only here temporarily. When West gets well enough not to need me I shall go on to another job.'

'But it won't be too far away, will it? If you live in the area...'

'No, I said that I *used* to, not that I do now. I have a flat in London, and I go to whichever part of the country that the job happens to be in.'

A look of deep disappointment came into Tim's eyes, but then he brightened. 'But West's bound to need you for months yet.'

She gave a peal of laughter. 'Hey, you're supposed to want your patients to get better, not to have them malingering for months on end.'

After that Maddy determinedly kept the conversation on safe ground, i.e. away from West, which wasn't always easy as Tim seemed rather in awe of him. He asked her again what *she* thought of West, but she laughingly refused to answer and he got the hint and didn't ask again, although he gave her a speculative glance. They lingered over their coffee, finding lots to talk about, as people who are just beginning to know one another and finding the other person to their liking always do. Tim told her about an arboretum he'd discovered not too far away, where the trees had started to turn to the gold of autumn, and he invited her to go there with him the next weekend.

Maddy hovered on the brink of a refusal, because she had the uneasy feeling that she was being deceitful. But surely her past was her own business. If she didn't want to tell Tim, who was after all a comparative stranger, then surely she didn't have to? Maybe when she knew him better, if they became friends. So she smiled and accepted and thanked him gracefully for dinner when he drove her back to High Beeches.

He had pulled up on the gravel driveway at the front of the house, and Maddy couldn't resist a quick look up at West's window where a light still shone out.

'Thanks for coming,' Tim returned. 'It's been a good evening. I'm glad we met.'

'Would you like to come in for a drink?'

'Thanks, but I can see that Mrs Marriott's bridge party is still on, so I won't intrude.'

'Oh, Laura won't mind, and we can always go in West's study.'

Tim looked at her in surprise. 'You're on first-name terms with Mrs Marriott?'

Annoyed with herself for the slip, Maddy said, 'Yes, she asked me to call her that and told me to make myself at home.'

'Did you know her as well, then, when you lived round here?'

'Yes, slightly. Well, if you won't come in I'll say goodnight, then. And thanks again for a lovely evening.'

She went to get out of the car, but Tim put a restraining hand on her arm, then leant forward and kissed her. Maddy stiffened and only slowly relaxed, accepting his kiss, but not returning it. She tried to be sensible, to realise this was only a harmless goodnight kiss that meant nothing, but she couldn't feel at ease and she lifted her head as soon as she could.

'Maddy,' Tim said thickly, 'I can't wait a whole week before I see you again. Couldn't you come out for a drink or something before then?'

'I don't know.' She hesitated, not wanting to get involved, but Tim was persistent and eventually she agreed to meet him for a snack lunch in Aberton, where he had his practice, on the following Wednesday.

Reluctantly, he let her go then, but not before he'd kissed her again, a lingering kiss that Maddy had to break.

'Hey,' she admonished him. 'We'll have all Laura's bridge guests coming out and catching us.' And she determinedly said goodnight again and got out of the car, letting herself into the house without waiting to see him off.

She had been right, Laura's bridge party was just coming to an end, the players counting out their wins and losses and bemoaning the grand slam they bid and almost made, just like fishermen talking of 'the one that got away'. Several of them knew Maddy from the past and greeted her amicably enough for Laura's sake, whatever their private feelings towards her were. Meeting people that she had known was one of the things Maddy had been afraid of in coming here, and she had made no attempt to look up any of her old friends since she'd arrived. Not that many of them had kept in touch with her; they mostly so admired West that they had blamed her for the break-up and had cut her dead. At first this had hurt her dreadfully, especially when it was by women whom she'd looked on as good and close friends. There had only been one or two who really understood, but they were married to racing drivers themselves—or were their widows—and they knew what hell it was for themselves.

But what had really hurt were the two occasions, after she'd left West, when the husbands of two of her friends had called on her at the hotel where she was staying before she started working for the agency. Both episodes had been repugnantly similar; she had welcomed each as the friend she thought he was, and he had begun by saying he was completely on her side, offering any help he could. Then he had invited her out for dinner, but afterwards took it for granted that there was only one way a lonely woman wanted to be comforted. The memories still made Maddy feel slightly sick, and she had vowed that she would never leave herself open to a similar approach again. Even now her manner towards Laura's friends was reserved, whereas in the past she had always been open and welcomed them into her home.

When they'd gone she helped Laura to clear up, and they chatted over a drink of hot chocolate before

Laura went up to bed. Maddy stayed up to watch a video programme that she'd taped, and then quietly followed her.

West was still awake. She saw the light under his door and hesitated, reluctant to go in. But her training overcame her own inclinations, and she tapped gently on his door and quietly opened it in the faint hope that he might have fallen asleep with the light on. He hadn't, of course; he was sitting up in bed with a large pad in front of him on which he was writing. For a moment he went on writing, ignoring her, not even bothering to look up as she came up to his bedside. But the tension in the room was so strong that Maddy felt as if she was walking into the lair of a dangerous animal. She felt an overwhelming desire to turn and run, but somehow stood her ground and spoke as lightly as possible. 'Hi, how are you?'

Only when his sentence was finished did West raise his eyes to look at her. 'As you see,' he gestured towards his legs sardonically.

Refusing to rise to the bait, she said, 'You seem busy.'

'Yes, I am. I've been working out a new timetable for my therapy and exercises. Here, read it.'

Maddy shot him a look under her lashes, but took the pad from him and began to read. Her eyebrows went up almost at once. '*Three* sessions a day?'

'For the time being. In a couple of weeks I'll put it up to four, I think.'

'*You* won't put it up to anything. May I remind you that I'm the expert. We can extend the present sessions by ten minutes or so, but you're far from ready to do a whole hour more. You've got to give your body time to heal.'

'I'll be the judge of how much I can or cannot do,' he corrected her brusquely.

Maddy opened her mouth to argue, but realised that that was what he wanted and shut it again. Handing the pad back to him she said, 'We'll discuss it some other time. I'm tired.'

'Really? Tiring was it, snogging in the car like a couple of lovesick teenagers?' His voice grew bitter. 'Or was it going back to his place beforehand that's made you so tired?'

Maddy's face tightened and she was about to make a heated denial, but West's arrogance suddenly got to her and she decided to pay him back a little, so she said offhandedly, 'Possibly, but I had quite a bit to drink first.'

His eyes came up to stare into hers. 'First.'

'Over dinner,' she explained nonchalantly.

'So he took you out to dinner before you went back with him?'

'Yes, to a new restaurant where the Bacchus wine bar used to be. Do you know it? The food was quite good.'

'No, I can't say that I do.' West was gazing at her intently, not quite sure how to take it. 'You never used to drink very much,' he said slowly.

'No, but I do quite a lot of things now that I didn't before.'

West's jaw hardened perceptibly. 'I don't think I believe you.'

'Don't you?' she asked in amusement. 'Can this be the confident West Marriott who's always so sure of himself—and so certain that anyone who doesn't agree with him is a fool?'

'All right. Tell me what his place is like.'

'He has a flat above the surgery.'

'I know that—and so does everyone else. What's it like inside, in the sitting-room for instance?'

Maddy gave a low laugh. 'I don't remember much about the *sitting*-room.'

A flash of pure rage shone in West's eyes, and he shot out a hand to grab her, but then stopped himself. 'You vixen,' he grated. 'You're just trying to rile me. You weren't there at all. Were you?'

She laughed again. 'You'll never know, will you?'

'But I can guess.'

'Guess away. You can hardly expect me to kiss and tell, now, can you? That wouldn't be playing the game.'

'A game, is that all it is to you now?' Unable to hold back any longer, West reached out and closed his hand over her wrist.

A little breathlessly, Maddy retorted, 'Of course it's a game. Wasn't it a game for you every time you got in a car and raced? Only for you it stopped being a game on the day you crashed! But you couldn't face up to that, could you? If you couldn't walk and race, then you didn't want to live.'

'Damn you, I'll walk again—and I'll race,' West yelled at her.

'Yes, that's right,' she shot back at him fiercely. 'Then it will all be a game again, won't it? Until you crash the next time. But I had enough of your game, West. I grew up—and now I play my own games.'

He stared at her, then shook her wrist violently. 'Tell me,' he shouted harshly. 'Did you go back with him?'

'Why? What is it to you? The way you're going on, anyone would think you still cared. Or is it just that you can't get used to the idea that I don't belong to you any more?'

His fingers suddenly bit into her wrist so hard that she had to bite off a gasp of pain, but West's face went ashen as the colour drained from it. 'Yes,' he admitted, his voice filled with inner rage and despair. 'Yes, God help me, I still care. You're mine! You'll always be mine. And to hell with the divorce.' He lunged for her, but Maddy stepped quickly back.

'No!' she cried out in horror. 'No, I don't want that. Can't you understand? I've finished with you. I didn't want to come here, and as soon as this is over I want to leave and never see you again.'

CHAPTER FIVE

WEST'S temperature had risen when Maddy took it the next morning, but she merely noted it on his chart and made no comment. They were back to icy politeness again, but after the morning therapy session he asked her to go down to his study and bring him all the household accounts. Maddy passed this on to Laura, who'd been dealing with them.

'Oh, how wonderful,' Laura beamed. 'If he wants to do that, he must really be taking an interest in life again. I'll go and sort them out at once.'

She went off happily and Maddy took the dogs for a walk, coming back to find Sandy taking the last cut of the lawn before the winter. He stopped when he saw her and said, 'How's West this morning? He was really fretful last night. Nothing I could do would keep him interested for more than a few minutes at a time.'

'He's convalescent,' Maddy explained, carefully avoiding the real reason. 'He's still got as much mental energy as he had before, but not the strength, so he gets frustrated quickly.'

'Well, if he could get out of bed I'd say he got out the wrong side of it yesterday. How's he progressing?'

'Very well. Slowly but very surely. As long as he doesn't try to overdo it, he'll be fine.'

'You reckon he'll walk again, then?'

'His spine isn't damaged, so there's no real reason why he shouldn't. It's just that his leg and hip bones were so badly broken that they might never mend enough to support him. But I'm giving them as much therapy as I can to help strengthen them.'

'If there's a chance that he'll walk, then West will make it,' Sandy declared positively. 'He always was a fighter—and stubborn with it.' He gave her a sudden grin. 'Or at least, he's fighting now that you've come home. He seemed to change overnight, then. Do you reckon you two will get back together?' he asked hopefully.

But his face fell when Maddy said firmly, 'No, there's absolutely no chance of that.'

'That'll set West back a lot when he finds out.'

'He knows already. I'm only here until he gets well.' She went to turn away, but then hesitated. 'Have you nearly finished, Sandy? I thought perhaps you might like a cup of tea.'

'Always willing to stop for a cup of tea,' he grinned, and followed her into the kitchen.

Laura was upstairs with West still and Mrs Campbell didn't work at the weekends, so they had the place to themselves. Maddy put two large mugs of tea on the kitchen table and sat down opposite Sandy. For a while they talked about the dogs and the garden, but then Sandy gave her a quizzical look. 'Something on your mind, is there?'

She gave a little grimace. 'Very much so. In fact, it's been on my mind for quite some time.' Putting down her mug, Maddy looked across at Sandy intently. 'I'm sorry if what I'm going to ask upsets you, but you're the only person I *can* ask. Were you—were you there when West crashed?'

'So that's it.' Sandy's bushy eyebrows drew into a frown, but then he nodded. 'Yes, I was there,' he acknowledged abruptly. '*I* was always there when he raced.'

He said it rather accusingly, silently implying that she should have been there too. Maddy bit her lip, but said steadily, 'What happened? Would you tell me, please?'

'Didn't you see it on the television news? They showed it often enough that day.'

'No.' She shook her head and looked away. 'It came on, but I—I couldn't watch it.'

Sandy gave a swift glance at her averted face, saw the pulse beating in her throat, and his eyes softened. 'What do you want to know?'

'All of it. All you can remember.'

'I don't think I'll ever forget it.' He paused, his mind going back, then said in a crisp tone that disguised his feelings, 'It was about three-quarters of the way through the race. It had been raining but it had stopped, so most of the cars still had their wet tyres on. There was a battle between West and another guy for second place. West was faster but the other driver wouldn't let him pass, and it was a very twisting track where there weren't many opportunities to overtake. I could hear West cursing him over the radio from where I was in the pits. The team manager was telling him to cool it, but West could see his chance of winning slipping away from him. The driver in front kept taking the inside line, shutting him out, but then West saw a chance and went to go through on the inside on a bend.' Sandy's voice slowed and his knuckles showed white as he gripped his mug. 'He almost made it, but at the last minute the other driver realised what was happening and tried to close the gap. They must have touched—it's not absolutely certain, but most people agree that they must have touched. Then West's car went up in the air and somersaulted twice. It came down on its nose, that's why his legs were so badly injured. It started to flame,' he went on, unable to keep the emotion out of his voice now. 'But the stewards were there in seconds and put the fire out. They were bloody marvellous. Putting their own lives at risk like that.' He stopped, too overcome to go on and took a deep swig of his almost cold tea.

Maddy understood his feelings, understood them only too well, but there were more things she wanted to know, and it was best to ask them now. 'Did they get him out straight away?'

'No, he was trapped. It took us over half an hour before we could get him free.'

'We? You were there helping?'

He nodded briefly. 'Yes, I was there.'

Maddy lowered her head before the pain in his eyes. 'Was—was he conscious?'

'Some of the time. But then they got a doctor and he put him out.'

She hadn't intended to ask the next question, but couldn't resist it. 'Did he—say anything when he was conscious?'

Sandy shot her a look under his frowning brows. 'He might have done.'

So he still couldn't forgive her enough to tell her. Maddy didn't press him, but asked, 'What sort of a mood was he in that day?'

'Mood?' The question clearly puzzled him. 'Uptight, I suppose, but then he always is—was a bit before a race. Impatient to start and get going.'

'But not more so than usual?'

He frowned again, was about to speak and then changed his mind, shaking his head.

'Please tell me, Sandy. I—I have to know. Ever since his crash it's always been at the back of my mind that he—that he *wanted* to crash.'

'Wanted to!' Sandy stared at her. 'Are you saying that he did it deliberately?'

'No! No, of course not. But you said he was angry; he didn't used to get angry when he drove. West was always very cool, very...' She groped for a word. 'Very professional about it.'

Sandy nodded reluctantly. 'Yes, you're right. He'd changed that last year or so. He'd become—obsessed with winning. It was as if nothing else mattered.'

'And he took risks that he shouldn't have done?' After a moment Sandy nodded silently, unwilling to say a word against West. 'And on the day he crashed— that was an unnecessary risk, wasn't it?'

'I suppose you could say that.'

Maddy bit her lip, and there was a heavy silence between them until she forced herself to ask the question that she knew she must. 'Was it because of me that he changed? Was it after I left him?'

Sandy's eyes came up to meet hers, cold and condemning. 'Of course it was,' he said roughly. 'What else could it have been?'

She nodded, her face white. 'I've always been afraid...' She looked down at her clenched fists. 'Was anyone else hurt? The other driver or the race stewards?'

'No. Just West.'

She stood up. 'Would you like another mug of tea?'

'No, thanks.' Sandy hesitated, then demanded harshly, 'Why didn't you go and see him when he was in hospital?'

'For the same reason that I left him; because I couldn't bear to see him hurt and in pain. I'm not—very brave where West is concerned, you see.'

He obviously didn't understand, but said grudgingly, 'Well, at least you're here now and doing what you can for him. If he does walk it will be thanks to you.'

She looked at him, her eyes over-bright. 'But if he does, he will go back to racing, won't he?'

Sandy nodded slowly. 'Aye, that's what he'll want.' He stood up, the thought weighing heavily on his mind. 'Thanks for the tea, I'd better go and finish the lawn.'

He went away, but Maddy stood for a long time staring out of the kitchen window, wondering if her leaving him had driven West to the one thing she had been so terribly afraid of.

West was very busy that afternoon, the next day and the day after, making several phone calls and writing letters, taking over the running of the house and his own business interests again. A task that Laura was only too thankful to hand over to him. She had taken it over because there had been no choice, and done it very efficiently, but it was something she certainly didn't enjoy. By the time Maddy took the dogs for a walk at about noon on Tuesday, there were so many letters that they had run out of stamps and she had to walk down to the sub-post office, which was rather a grand name for the very small partitioned-off counter in the village shop where the father of the proprietor took on the job of sub-postmaster.

It was the first time that Maddy had gone as far as the village since she'd been back, and she would have avoided it if she could, even though she chided herself for being over-sensitive. The whole village knew about West, of course; he was their local celebrity. And Maddy was quite sure that they all knew about her within a day of her return to High Beeches. Mrs Campbell, although an excellent housekeeper, wasn't above a comfortable gossip with her cronies. The shop was situated at the far end of the village, so she had to run the gauntlet of several people that she knew, some of whom looked away in embarrassment, although some nodded and two women actually stopped outside the shop to ask her how West was. They were members of the village tennis club, to which she and West had belonged, although she had played there far more than West. Before the divorce they had all been on first-name terms and had visited each other socially, but the two women had made it quite plain whose side they were on over the divorce. So now Maddy was rather offhand as she answered them.

'And you? How are you?' one asked. 'We were so pleased to hear that you were back with West.'

'Really?' Maddy raised an eyebrow. 'Who told you that?'

The woman looked taken aback at the direct question. 'Oh—I can't quite remember. It's just general knowledge.'

Maddy gave a honey-sweet smile. 'It's always so amusing when gossips get their facts wrong, isn't it? It makes the people who repeat it look so stupid.' And with another smile she went into the shop, feeling that she'd scored a very minor victory, but then realised what a petty one it was and felt ashamed.

The people in the shop were much nicer, sounding genuinely pleased to see her, and sending back a small gift for West: a box of his favourite mint chocolates.

Feeling in a much happier frame of mind, Maddy walked back to the house for lunch and found a strange car parked on the driveway.

'Who's here?' she asked Laura as she went into the kitchen.

'Mr Ambrose. The bank manager, you remember? It seems West called him this morning to talk over his financial affairs, and luckily he was free to come today. West's invited him to lunch,' she added, not quite so enthusiastically.

'Oh, dear. Can I help? Is he eating with us or with West?'

'With West. It doesn't really matter, but I would have liked a little more notice.'

'You should be used to West unexpectedly inviting or bringing people to a meal. He was always doing it when we were married. He brought his whole racing team back to dinner more than once.'

'Well, you may have allowed him to do that, Maddy, dear, but I didn't. If he wanted to entertain his friends at short notice, then I always insisted he took them out somewhere.'

Maddy smiled, remembering how Laura liked everything to be just so, but then she wondered if West had brought his friends back to an empty house after she had left him, and her face sobered. 'Is there anything I can do?' she asked again.

'No, I think Mrs Campbell and I have everything in hand.'

The bank manager didn't leave until nearly three-thirty, and Maddy immediately went up to give West his afternoon session. He was leaning back on his pillows, a brooding look on his hawklike face. There were several files of papers still on his bed and one of them was open. It looked like his bank statements. His eyes hardened when he looked at her and, although his face wasn't so gaunt now, she still had a fleeting but vivid impression of an Indian warrior. She had used to tease him about it, she remembered. But West was quite obviously in no mood for teasing now.

'It seems I'm much richer than I thought,' he remarked brusquely.

Maddy knew just what was coming, but still tried to divert him by briskly starting to pick up the files and saying, 'I really don't think we need to work on your arm any more. You said it wasn't paining you, so as long as you . . .'

'You heard me,' West broke in harshly, stopping her as she went to take the open file. 'Why haven't you cashed the alimony cheques I sent you?' He hit the file with the back of his hand. 'I put a lump sum into a separate account after we split up so that a cheque could be sent to you every month. It hasn't been touched. Not a penny of it!'

'I told you I didn't want any alimony.'

'Why? Isn't my money good enough for you?' He glared at her balefully, more deep-down angry than Maddy had ever seen him. 'Just what have you been living on?' he demanded.

'On my abilities as a nurse,' Maddy retorted. 'The thing you looked upon as an amusing hobby for me when I took it up.'

'Is that *why* you took it up—because you intended to leave me even as far back as that?'

Surprised that he should even think it, Maddy said quickly, 'No.' But then paused. 'At least, not consciously. It was something challenging to do. And I— I needed something. I couldn't get a job round here as a physio—so I took up nursing.'

'And just how did you manage—after you'd so proudly spurned my money? Intent on turning yourself into a martyr, were you?'

'No, I was not!' Maddy's hands balled into fists at her sides. 'You spent a great deal of money on me while we were married. I'm not going to go on taking from you when we're divorced. Call it pride or whatever you like, but I needed to make my own way.'

But West was in no way appeased. Grimly he said, 'And is that why you left behind all the jewellery I gave you?'

'I didn't think that I had the right to them any more. I . . .'

'For God's sake! You thought you had the right to walk out on me, didn't you? Don't I have any rights? Don't I have the right to provide for the woman I loved and was married to? Do I have to have everything I've ever given you thrown back in my face as if I'm some kind of leper?'

He was breathing heavily, his face white with anger, and Maddy began to be afraid for him.

'West, I'm not throwing it back at you,' she explained urgently. 'I'm extremely well paid. Really. And you don't spend much money when you're nursing, so I saved an awful lot. So much that I was able to put a deposit on my flat and...'

'And where did you live before you had it?' West cut in. 'At cheap hotels. With only a couple of suitcases to hold everything you had. And don't try to deny it,' he added harshly. 'I *know*. I made it my business to find out.'

'It was convenient,' Maddy protested. 'I couldn't heave trunkloads of things round to every nursing job I was sent to. And I didn't need very much.'

'But you felt the need for a flat,' West pursued doggedly.

'Yes, I needed a—a base. Somewhere to call home, I suppose.'

His eyes darkened. '*This* was your home. But rather than try and work things out between us, you went off to live in some cheap hovel of a hotel.'

'That isn't fair,' she burst out. 'You only knew one way of working things out, and that was for me to go on doing what *you* wanted.' She stopped abruptly. 'I'm not going to go all through that again. I didn't want to go on living your life, West, and there was no way I was going to take your money so that I could live mine.' And she firmly took the file from him and put it aside with the others. 'Now, let's get on with the therapy, shall we?'

West suddenly smiled maliciously. 'Well, at least you're taking my money for *that*.'

'Certainly. And I'm darn well earning it!'

After the therapy session Maddy steered clear of West, driving Laura out to see a film while Sandy sat with him.

'What *do* you think?' Laura remarked as they drove along. 'West has invited someone to visit him who will be staying overnight. Isn't that marvellous?'

'Great,' Maddy agreed. 'Who is it?'

'He just said a friend, but he'll be arriving on Thursday, so Mrs Campbell and I will have to be busy getting a room ready and shopping tomorrow.'

'I'm going into Aberton tomorrow if I can get anything for you,' Maddy offered. 'I have a hairdresser's appointment at eleven-thirty, and I thought I'd have lunch there and do some shopping.'

'Oh, good. I'll write out a list for you.'

The list turned out to be quite long, and Maddy was only half-way through it when it came time to go and meet Tim Roberts for lunch. He was waiting for her in the bar of the local pub, the Rose and Crown, in a position where he could keep an eye on the door. His eyes lit up when he saw her and he rose eagerly to his feet. 'Hello, Maddy,' he greeted her warmly as he took her hand. Then he drew her closer and kissed her on the cheek.

'Hey,' she protested, drawing quickly away. 'People will start talking.'

'Is that so bad?' he teased.

'You don't know how people gossip in small towns and villages.'

He bought her a drink and they sat down, Tim giving her a rather quizzical look when she moved to a table away from the window. 'I shouldn't have thought you were the type who was sensitive to what people said about them.'

'I suppose it depends what they say,' Maddy retorted, more tartly than she'd intended. She took a deep breath. 'Sorry, I didn't mean to sound ratty. How are you? Busy?'

'Not too bad. Most of the patients have got over the foreign bugs they picked up on holiday and haven't yet started on their winter ailments.'

Maddy laughed, glad that the slight tension had eased. 'It must be absorbing to be a GP. I wish I could have trained to be a doctor.'

'Why didn't you?'

She shrugged. 'Not clever enough. And I'd got it into my head that I wanted to be a physiotherapist. I didn't realise how limiting that was until after I'd qualified.'

'What made you take up private nursing instead of working in a hospital?'

Maddy smiled. 'Well, it's better paid, for a start. And when I took it up I needed to—to get away for a while, to have a change of scene. And it's nice to be able to have a complete break between jobs.'

'Yes, I can see that,' he agreed. 'And I should imagine the work is certainly a lot easier than in a hospital.'

'One patient instead of twenty to take care of. That's certainly true. But how many do you have?'

'Oh, hundreds,' Tim laughed. 'But luckily they don't all get ill at once.'

'Don't you be too sure,' Maddy warned teasingly. 'You might yet have an epidemic on your hands.'

'Well, if I do, I shall certainly demand that you come and be my head nurse,' Tim laughed. He smiled at her warmly. 'As a matter of fact, I know of a private nursing home only a few miles from here that will be on the lookout for a nurse to take the place of one who's leaving to get married in three months' time. You wouldn't be interested, would you? It would mean that you could stay in this area.'

Maddy shook her head decisively. 'No, I don't think it would suit me. I've come to like being independent.'

A look of disappointment came into Tim's eyes, but the barmaid called out their order number just then and he went up to collect their food, and after that both of them made an effort to talk on impersonal subjects, so that the rest of lunch passed pleasantly enough.

At two Maddy excused herself to go and get the rest of Laura's shopping, bidding Tim a friendly goodbye. But now she almost wished that she wasn't seeing him again on Sunday. It was quite obvious that he was greatly attracted to her, and Maddy could see that what she had thought would be only a pleasant friendship and a means of making West jealous could quite easily become very involved. And involvement was the last thing she wanted.

One of the items on her list was a new pair of pyjamas for West, and she spent some time finding and choosing a pair that she thought he would really like. In the end Maddy bought a pair in pale blue silk with a darker blue piping. For a moment she was tempted to have them gift-wrapped and give them to him herself, but decided against it. She didn't want to have her offering sneered at—or taken as a sign that she still loved him.

Maddy sighed as she drove home, her head filled with West's admission that he still cared about her. It was something she'd tried to put out of her mind, believing that it was only West's subconscious refusal to accept her rejection of him. Even at the time he hadn't taken her seriously at first, constantly writing to her through her solicitors and trying to get her to live with him again. Perhaps he still loved her, as much as he could love anything apart from racing, but Maddy was sure that he had tried to make her go back to him purely because he couldn't stand the thought of failure. And it certainly hadn't done his he-man image any good, either. But then she remembered the anger and despair in his voice when he'd said that he cared. As if it had been dragged out of him against his will.

She sighed again, feeling completely mixed up about him. But then she hardened her heart, thinking that nothing had changed, especially West. That was why she had instantly rejected him yet again. An instinctive fear of the past repeating itself leading her to say what she had, cruel though it was. But at least it was the truth. My God, it was. And far better to have it out in the open than for West to start getting any ideas that she'd come back to look after him because she wanted to get together again.

West approved of the pyjamas. He was full of purpose that day, working hard at his exercises and having Mrs Campbell give his room a thorough clean—not that it really needed it. And he wanted to know what they were giving him and his guest for lunch and dinner tomorrow, and he ordered Sandy to keep the dogs out of the way, although they had become almost permanent fixtures in his room now.

'And do you know,' Laura exclaimed when she was telling Maddy all this, 'he insisted that I put some flowers in the guest bedroom.'

'But you would have done that anyway, surely.'

'I know. But West has never bothered to show any concern about it before. He always left all the details to me.'

'Or to me,' Maddy agreed, and wondered who on earth West had invited to stay. Perhaps another racing driver, she thought. Or even—her breath caught—or perhaps he'd invited one of his old racing sponsors to see if he could get backing again once he was on his feet. Maddy's blood felt suddenly cold in her veins and she became convinced that she was right. Why else would West not tell them who was coming? Cold changed to heat as she began to feel angry, knowing that to West it was a sure way of hitting back at her. Her mouth thinned grimly. But there was no guarantee yet that West would ever be able to sit in a racing car again. And no sponsor in his right mind was going to help him, not at least until he was able to walk again.

So she was feeling rather sardonic when she went into his room late that evening to make sure West had everything he needed for the night. He was doing a crossword puzzle in the paper, a frown of concentration between his brows.

'Tut, tut,' she admonished him. 'Shouldn't you be getting your beauty sleep, ready for tomorrow?'

His left eyebrow rose at her tone. 'Why say that, when you don't even know who I've invited?'

'Oh, but I can guess,' she answered in sharp mockery.

West's eyes narrowed. 'Can you now? And just who do you think it is?'

She hesitated for a moment, but was so sure she was right that she said, 'Someone to do with racing, of course.'

West relaxed against his pillows, a small smile on his lips. 'What makes you think that?'

'Well, isn't it? After all, what other friends do you have? Your whole world was wrapped up in racing.' She perched on the edge of the bed, watching his face. 'You keep telling me that you can't wait to get back to it. And I think that the person who's coming tomorrow is someone you hope will help you.'

'This is fascinating. And just who exactly do you think my guest is—my team manager, perhaps?'

'Possibly.' There was something in his voice that made her pause, but she thought it was suppressed annoyance at being found out, so she said, 'Or could it be a sponsor?'

'Ah. So that's the way your mind's working.' He gave a short laugh. 'Ironic, isn't it; you working to get me back on my feet so that I can race again, when it's the one thing you're so afraid of?'

'I'm not afraid of it now.'

'No?' His blond brows rose in disbelief. 'That's hardly the way you react whenever I mention it. I'd say you were very much afraid of it.'

'Which is why you mention it so often,' Maddy observed sarcastically. 'But you're wrong. I'm not afraid for you. I just hate the idea of—the waste of it all. Of getting you through all this suffering, only to have it all happen again.'

'You seem very sure that it will happen again,' West said sneeringly.

'Yes, I am. Because you'll still have the same attitude towards it, the obsession to win and to hell with the risks.'

His grey eyes darkened as he studied her face. 'And just what makes you so damn sure of that statement? I was always reckoned to be a cool and level-headed driver.'

'Yes, perhaps you were—once. But you were hardly driving responsibly on the day you crashed, were you?'

West's lips curled into a sneer. 'What an authority on my psyche you've suddenly become. And what makes you so certain, I wonder?' he demanded suspiciously.

Maddy hesitated, realising that she couldn't betray Sandy's confidence. 'I saw it on television,' she lied. 'You were driving like a madman.'

His nose narrowed in a snort of derision. 'Don't tell me you were thinking that I'd gone to pieces because you'd left me.' He laughed scornfully. 'If you must know, I'd had a row with the driver in front of me the night before at a party. Over a girl, as a matter of fact. We almost came to blows, but they pulled us apart and he vowed to keep me out of the race. I didn't intend to let him. And when he tried to block me I saw my chance to pass him, but he deliberately sent me off the track.'

Maddy didn't believe him for a moment. If that had really happened after a public row, there would have been hell to pay for the other driver. So she merely said, 'You didn't used to go to parties the night before a race.'

'Ah, but that was when I was married to you. I stupidly felt that I had to be responsible—and faithful,' he added tauntingly. 'But once the shackles were broken I was free to do as I damn well pleased.'

She looked at him for a moment, then said calmly, 'I don't believe you. Not any of it.'

'No? But then I don't believe you, either.'

'About what?'

'When you say you're not afraid of me going back to racing.' His mouth thinned. 'You can't bear even the thought of it.'

Maddy stood up. 'But you're wrong. I was only afraid of it when I was in love with you. Now,' she shrugged. 'Now you can go to hell whichever way you choose.'

A sharp flame of anger lit his eyes, but West said silkily, 'Well, we'll find out the truth of that when my—racing friend arrives tomorrow, won't we?' His gaze held hers for a moment, but then he suddenly laughed again, in real amusement this time.

Maddy left him to his mirth, but there was a frown of puzzlement between her brows as she wondered just what he found so darn funny.

She found out just over twelve hours later when the doorbell rang and she went to open it because Laura and Mrs Campbell were busy in the kitchen. She glimpsed a taxi outside through the porch window, and realised that West's mystery guest had arrived. Eagerly she opened the door, laying bets in her mind on who it would be, but stood, thunderstruck, when not a man but a very curvy blonde stood on the threshold.

'Hi,' the woman said with an attractive American accent. 'I'm Delia Morgan. I guess West is expecting me.'

CHAPTER SIX

MADDY was so taken aback that she could only stand and stare, for once lost for words. But Delia Morgan was looking at her in growing puzzlement and said, 'Say, don't I know you? Aren't you—I mean, weren't you—West's wife? But of course you were,' she went on when Maddy didn't speak. 'I don't suppose you remember, but we met once when you came to America with West.'

'Yes, of course. Won't you come in?' Maddy said stiffly, finding her voice at last.

'I'll just pay off the cab; I wanted to be sure this was the right place.'

Yes, Maddy thought as she watched her turn away, I remember you very well. It had only been six months or so after their marriage that West had taken her to New York on a trip that was to be part business, part pleasure. While they were there they'd been invited to a cocktail party by someone he knew—from the racing world, of course. It had been one of those sophisticated, cosmopolitan-type parties, with people whose names she recognised from the literary and theatrical world as well as from racing.

It was the first time Maddy had attended such a glossy party and she was thoroughly enjoying it, but then her hostess took her away from West's side to introduce her to a quite well-known author whose books Maddy admired.

Maddy was still in the group round the author when she heard a woman's voice call, 'West!' in delighted surprise. It was Delia Morgan. And when Maddy looked round she had just put her arms round West's neck and was giving him a warm kiss of greeting. A kiss so warm and so close that it was perfectly obvious that the two had been a lot more than just friends. West had put a familiar hand on Delia's hip for a moment as he returned the kiss, and had only laughingly pulled away. She had walked over to them then and he had introduced them, an amused smile on his lips when Maddy put a possessive arm through his. That night, when they had got back to their hotel, she had demanded to know whether he and Delia had been lovers, and he had admitted it at once. 'You can hardly have expected me *not* to have had women before I met you, now can you?' he had said reasonably, his eyes mocking her jealousy.

'Why not? I'd never been with anyone else.'

'Ah, but it's different for a man.'

Maddy had picked up a pillow and thrown it at him. 'Don't give me that. You louse.'

Putting up his arm to avoid a flying hairbrush, West had grabbed her and pulled her down on the bed. 'But a man has to have some experience,' he had pointed out, his eyes darkening. 'Or else he wouldn't know how to do this—and this.' So what had started as a row had turned into yet another night of ecstatic, sensual happiness for them both.

Delia had only brought one suitcase with her, which she put down in the hall. She again looked at Maddy searchingly. 'Er—say, did I get it wrong? I heard that you and West got divorced a while back.'

'Yes, that's right, we did,' Maddy admitted, trying to keep her voice neutral. 'But we haven't got back together, if that's what you're wondering. I'm a nurse, so I—I've come home to look after West until he's well again, that's all.'

'Oh, I see.' But Delia gave her a rather calculating look. 'How is West? He sounded fine on the phone.'

'Why don't you go up and see for yourself? I'm sure he's looking forward to seeing you.'

'Sure, in just a minute.' Delia hesitated, then said, 'You looked real surprised to see me. Didn't West tell you I was coming to stay?'

Her lips drawing into a thin smile, Maddy answered, 'Oh, you know West; he always likes to give people these little surprises.'

Delia looked as if she was going to say something else, but Laura came out into the hall, her face as astonished as Maddy's had been when she saw that their visitor was a woman. But she recovered quickly and came forward to be introduced. Maddy immediately excusing herself and leaving Laura to deal with the situation. She went into West's study, trying not to listen to the murmur of voices in the hall, but after only a few minutes Laura came in and she heard Delia running lightly up the stairs to West's room.

'Well! What a surprise,' Laura said unnecessarily. 'I wonder who she is?'

'A very old friend of West's,' Maddy answered flatly. 'Before my time. I met her once in America.'

'Oh, I see.' There was a wealth of understanding in Laura's voice. 'Is she married?'

'I'm not sure. I think she's divorced.'

'Like you, then,' Laura reminded her gently.

'Yes. Like me,' Maddy agreed, and smiled without humour.

'I should imagine it's a very difficult thing to come to terms with, being divorced. You're neither one thing nor the other, not a spinster nor a widow. A sort of in-between state.'

'Yes,' Maddy agreed with an edge of bitterness in her voice. 'You're used. Second-hand. And a failure, too. And that's the worst part, knowing that you've failed at the most important thing in your life.'

'You chose to leave West,' Laura reminded her.

'Yes, I know, but that only makes it harder.' She raised troubled eyes to the older woman's. 'But I *had* to, Laura. Please believe that. I—I just couldn't take any more.' Her voice broke and she abruptly stood up and went to the window. 'I beg your pardon. You're West's mother; I shouldn't be saying this to you.'

'My dear child.' Laura came to put a comforting hand on her shoulder. 'I love him, too. And I do understand—now.'

'Yet you blamed me for leaving him.'

'Yes, I'm afraid I did. I suppose I thought that you ought to have been stronger. As strong as West.' She sighed. 'But now I see that I was as much to blame as West was. I should have realised what was happening and added my voice to yours.'

Maddy laughed. 'That would only have made him even more determined to carry on.'

She turned round and found Laura looking at her hesitatingly. 'I suppose I shouldn't ask, but are you still in love with him?'

'Yes, of course I am,' Maddy answered shortly. 'I've never stopped loving him.'

'Well, then, couldn't you possibly...? Now that he won't be able to race again...'

But Maddy shook her head vehemently. 'No, there's no way we can ever get back together. Don't you see, he still *wants* to race, and he will if he can. I couldn't live with him if he did. Especially after seeing him like this. And if he doesn't get well enough to race and I went back to him, it would be as if I'd won. And I don't think he'd ever forgive me for that.'

Laura nodded reluctantly. 'Yes, I see. But I'm sure that he's still in love with you, Maddy. He changed so completely when you came here to nurse him.'

Maddy gave a disbelieving laugh. 'You think so— when he has Delia Morgan upstairs with him right now?'

'Oh, that.' Laura smiled. 'You ought to be pleased. You tried to make him jealous—now it's his turn.'

The idea hadn't occurred to Maddy before, but now she remembered that it was only *after* she went out with Tim that West had got busy on the phone. The thought cheered her, but she didn't help to carry the lunch trays up to West's room. No way was she going to wait on his old flame.

After lunch, Laura went up to show Delia to her room, and a little later the American girl came downstairs for a while. 'Hi,' she said, opening the sitting-room door. 'Is it OK if I come in?'

'Yes, of course.' Maddy got up from the chair where she had been doing some sewing for Sandy. 'Can I get you a drink or anything?'

'No, thanks. What gorgeous dogs. Are they yours?'

'We used to share them, but now they're West's.'

'This is a real pretty place,' Delia remarked, going over to the french windows. 'Did you live here long?'

'About four years. Do go out in the garden if you'd like to,' she added, resuming her sewing.

'Perhaps some other time.' Delia turned to face her. 'West tells me he intends to go back to racing. Is that possible? Wasn't he too badly injured?'

'If he says he will, then that's what he'll do,' Maddy answered shortly, snipping off a cotton.

'But is it definite? I mean, you're his nurse, you're the one who should know.'

'What do you want, a detailed medical report?' Maddy stood up, tired of having questions thrown at her and wanting to ask a few of her own. 'Are you in England on holiday?'

'Why, yes. I'm staying with some relatives in Hampshire for a couple of months.'

'How lucky for West. I wonder how he found out that you were here. Perhaps a mutual friend told him.'

'No,' Delia's chin came up. 'As a matter of fact I wrote to him a couple of weeks ago and told him I was over. We are—old friends, you know.'

'Yes, he told me,' Maddy replied calmly, and felt a small stab of satisfaction at the other girl's surprised look. 'I suppose now that you're in England you'll be going the rounds of all your old friends over here. Visiting them, that is,' she added innocently.

Delia's lips tightened. 'If I hadn't thought the field was open, I wouldn't have come.'

Maddy dropped her eyes. 'Yes, it's open,' she said hollowly. 'Wide open. As a matter of fact, you're the first person he's asked to visit him.'

'But you haven't exactly lost interest yourself, have you?'

'He's a hard man to forget.' Maddy walked over to the door. 'But I'm sure you won't let that stand in your way.'

'No, I won't. If I decide that West is what I want.'

Maddy turned in sudden anger. 'Just don't play around with his emotions, that's all. He's suffered enough.'

'Well, from what I hear, you were the one to make him suffer, so I really don't think it's up to you to start making conditions, do you?' Delia reached past her to open the door. 'Is that Sandy I hear coming down? Why, yes, it is. I'll go back up to West, then. He told me to hurry right back.'

Hastily fetching her jacket, Maddy whistled the dogs and went outside. A very light rain was falling, not much more than a feeling of dampness carried on the wind that plucked at her hair. She had a terrible feeling that she had just made an utter fool of herself and played right into West's hands. If he'd wanted to make her jealous he had definitely succeeded, which was stupid, utterly stupid. And she certainly had no right to be rude to Delia because of it. But then, Delia had asked so many questions about West's condition, almost as if she was weighing up whether it would be worth making a play for him again. She had seemed so—shallow. Moodily Maddy picked up a stick and threw it as far as she could, the dogs setting off in joyful pursuit. Damn Delia, Maddy thought. If she hurts West again . . .

A car turned into the driveway and she ran to catch the dogs, but it was only Tim, paying his weekly visit to West.

'Hello. This is lucky. Were you just going for a walk?' He got out of the car and slipped his arm around her waist. 'What's the matter? You look fed-up.'

'What? Oh, no, nothing. I'm fine.'

'Sure? I have a fantastic bedside manner, you know, if you're feeling unwell.'

Maddy laughed. 'If I were your patient, you'd have to keep your distance.'

'There is that. No, definitely don't get ill; I don't want some other doctor looking down that lovely throat of yours.' He smiled at her. 'That's better, you look much happier now.'

'Ah, so that was an example of your bedside manner, was it?'

'Definitely.' Bending forward, he kissed her on the lips. 'And this is another—especially for you.'

She smiled, but the dogs pulled at her and she said, 'I really ought to take them for their walk.'

'Can you hang on for ten minutes? I'll go and see West and then come with you.'

'You won't be very popular today; he has a visitor.'

'Really? Still, I don't suppose he will mind waiting outside for a few minutes. I won't be very long.'

'It isn't a he, it's a she,' Maddy told him in a detached tone.

'*Really?*' Tim glanced up at West's windows. 'Not his wife?'

'Oh, no.' Maddy smiled thinly. 'An old girlfriend, I believe. An American.'

'This I've got to see,' Tim declared. 'Can you wait for me?'

'The dogs are getting pretty impatient. Tell you what: I'll walk on down the lane towards the woods, and perhaps you can catch me up in the car if I haven't already turned off.'

'OK. Walk slowly,' he admonished, kissing her again.

Maddy didn't exactly hurry down the lane, but the dogs were eager to reach the woods where they would be let off their leads, so she didn't dawdle either. She unclipped their leashes and the dogs bounded off, sending up flurries of leaves that had started falling off the trees. Maddy followed them, walking quickly until she was out of sight of the lane. It wasn't so much that she didn't want to go for a walk with Tim, as that she wanted to be on her own. To think, to wonder why the hell she was putting herself through all this. West had recovered sufficiently now not to need a full-time nurse, not with Sandy and Laura to look after him, she reasoned. All he needed was a physio to come in and give him two sessions of treatment and exercise every day. She could leave, go back to London, or take on another case. But would that be keeping her promise to Laura?

With a heavy sigh, Maddy leaned against a tree-trunk, feeling far from happy. But she'd known that this job wasn't going to be easy, far from it, and she couldn't quit now, not when West was doing so well, physically. She tried to calculate how long it would be before he was back on his feet. Perhaps in another couple of weeks he might try to stand, then take a few steps on crutches a week or so after that if all was well. But she knew that it would be another couple of months at least after that before she would be able to even think of leaving, if she stayed to see the job through. One of the dogs came back with a stick in its mouth for her to throw, and she sent it whizzing through the air, hurled with all her frustrated anger. She would like to leave now, right now, because she didn't think she was going to be able to stand the look of triumphant mockery in West's eyes when she went to give him his therapy this afternoon. He had certainly played tit for tat in this jealousy game, and Maddy wasn't at all sure who had been angered the most.

It began to rain more heavily and she turned up her coat collar, tucking her hair inside. The dogs had chased a rabbit into its hole, and were barking so excitedly that they didn't come when she called them. By the time Maddy had rounded them up it was raining quite heavily, and she got thoroughly soaked as she hurried home.

She had a quick shower and changed, but there was no time to do more than rough-dry her hair before she had to go in and give West his treatment. Maddy grimaced at herself in the mirror. Her hair had gone into curls, and all she could do was fluff her fingers through them to make them stand away from her head more. She gave an inner groan; the one day when she ought to have looked her best. The curls so accentuated her high cheekbones that she resembled a gypsy. Compared to Delia she looked like a village rustic. But there was nothing for it, she would have to go in and face them.

At the door to West's room she halted, wondering suddenly whether she ought to knock. A feeling almost of hysteria hit her as she wondered what was the correct etiquette when you wanted to intrude on your ex-husband and his ex-mistress. Somebody ought to write a book about it, she thought dazedly, but then firmly pushed open the door and walked in.

Now that West's bed had been raised, they had brought up a couple of bar stools from downstairs, so that anyone with him would be at his level. Delia was perched on one of these but leaning forward, her elbow on West's bed, her head close to his. They turned when Maddy entered and she looked at West with chin high, expecting derision; but his face merely hardened and then he looked away.

Puzzled, Maddy turned to Delia. 'I expect West has told you that he has to have physiotherapy twice a day. It's time for his afternoon session now.'

Delia stood up at once. 'I guess I'll leave you to it, then. I'll go and talk go your mother for a while before I change for dinner.' She looked at West and laughed. 'We are changing for dinner, aren't we?'

'We most certainly are.' West smiled and held her hand for a moment before Delia left.

As soon as she'd gone, Maddy busied herself with getting her equipment ready, but she sneaked several glances at West under her lashes. She had expected him to be smug to say the least, to be taking a sadistic satisfaction in having sprung Delia on her, but he merely leaned against the bedhead, a withdrawn look on his angular features. 'Ready?' she asked him.

He nodded, and she peeled back the bedclothes as he lowered himself into a lying position. He was wearing swimming trunks as usual, because it was so much easier during the day. His scars were healing well, no longer a violent red but fading to pink. 'Are your hips paining you?' she asked, because she knew that it still hurt him to sit up for any length of time.

'Hardly at all.'

But Maddy saw the pinched look around his mouth and said, 'Don't sit up much more today.'

'Yes, Nurse,' West answered coldly, a bite in his voice.

She shot him a glance, but then quickly switched on the heat lamp and turned away, waiting.

There was a silence in the room, the only sounds the ticking of the clock and the patter of rain on the window. But the tension that grew in the silence was loud, shriekingly loud. Maddy bit her lip, determined not to break it, determined not to look at him, so it was West who said at last, in a harsh statement that sounded more like an accusation, 'You've been out in the rain.'

Startled, she said, 'Why, yes, I took the dogs for a walk.'

'Where did you go?'

'Down to the wood. I nearly always take them there, just as we used to when . . .' She broke off, realising that this wasn't the time to reawaken old memories.

But West finished it for her. 'When we took them for walks together.' He was silent again for a moment, then said harshly, 'You look ridiculously young with your hair like that. Almost as you did when I first knew you. You wore it curly then.'

'Did I? Yes, I suppose I did. But I was only about twenty then. Soon I'll be twenty-seven.'

West turned his head to look at her fully. 'That's right, it's your birthday quite shortly, isn't it? Next month. And do you intend to celebrate?'

'I really hadn't thought about it,' Maddy admitted truthfully. 'Maybe I'll treat myself to a bottle of champagne.'

'And who are you going to share it with?' West asked, his mouth curling into a sneer. 'Tim Roberts?'

Maddy stiffened, understanding now. 'Perhaps. Perhaps I won't share it with anyone.'

'Oh, come now. Are you trying to make me feel sorry for you?'

Suddenly angry, Maddy shot at him, 'Pity is the last thing I want from you!'

West stared at her for a moment, then said, 'Or I from you—or anyone.'

'Well, you certainly won't get it from me, because you brought this on yourself.'

'Bad luck didn't come into it, I suppose?' He lifted a hand. 'No, there's no need for you to answer that; if I hadn't been racing it wouldn't have happened, of course. Has it ever occurred to you that I might just as easily have had an accident driving on ordinary roads?'

'I hardly think you would have tried to overtake on a bend on an ordinary road,' she rejoined tartly.

His mouth thinned into a mirthless smile. 'You seem to have an answer to everything nowadays.'

'I learnt from a very experienced source.'

West lay silent while she adjusted the lamp, her body stiff with anger. Then he said abruptly, 'Did Dr Roberts catch you up?'

'What makes you think he intended to?'

He laughed shortly. 'Because today's must have
been the shortest doctor's visit on record. And after
the way I saw him pawing you out in the garden, it
didn't take much to work out just why he was in such
an all-fired hurry.' His jaw thrusting forward, West
said, 'Are you going out with him again?'

'Yes. He's taking me out on Sunday,' Maddy
answered coolly. 'And if you're interested, I had lunch
with him yesterday, too.'

'But you haven't yet told him the truth?'

'I haven't lied to him.'

'You know what I mean. He might feel differently
about you if he found out that you were my wife. He
might even have some moral quibbles about pursuing
the affair right under my nose.'

'It isn't an affair,' Maddy protested.

'Shouldn't you have added—"yet"?'

'No! For God's sake, West, I hardly know him.'

'But you like him?'

'Yes. Yes, I do. He's very—nice,' she answered
inadequately.

'Ah, nice! Now I see the attraction. You mean safe.
Unlikely even to drive over sixty miles an hour, and
certain never to take any risks. Yes, to a coward like
you he must be irresistible.'

Goaded, Maddy retorted, 'Well, as you're completely the opposite you should be very happy with
Delia. You should suit her fine—just so long as you
get yourself well enough to get into a racing car again,
of course.' And she switched off the lamp and began
to rub cream on to his legs, not at all gently.

'Ouch!' West had begun to laugh, but gave a wince of pain. 'I won't ask you to explain that remark. Women always get bitchy when they're jealous.'

'Huh! You're a fine one to talk, you're jealous as hell of Tim.'

'Yes, I am.' Suddenly serious, West shot out a hand and caught hers. 'But not the way you think. You flatter yourself if you think I'm jealous of *you*. No, I'm jealous of him,' he said forcefully, 'being able to walk, and chat up a girl. Of being able to work, and live and love, instead of being shackled to this damn bed for the rest of my life!'

He let her go and turned away, his body trembling. Maddy stood still for a long moment, realising that he was still far from convinced about his chances, that nothing she had yet done had got to him enough to give him the indomitable will to get well. How deep, then, must have been his conviction that he would never walk again. Automatically she applied the suckers and turned on the Interferaction machine, its gentle vibration covering the empty silence.

She went on working on his legs, but didn't speak until she was packing up the machine, then said, 'I've already told you that there's a good chance that you'll walk again eventually. Maybe sooner than you think. And what's to stop you from working? There must be loads of jobs you could do right now, from your bed. All you have to do is to turn the room into an office.'

West turned himself over on to his back and she put the pillows behind him so that he could sit up again. 'Really?' His tone was heavy with sarcasm.

'You seem to know so much about it; what do you suggest?'

'Well, you could do some charity work for a start. There are lots of people a hell of a lot worse off than you who need help.'

He gave her a malevolent look and said, 'And just how would I set about doing that?'

'By using your brain,' Maddy retorted. 'You do keep it in your head and not in your legs, don't you? Or did that get injured in the crash, too?'

She turned, angrily, to leave him, but West said, 'There was one thing you missed out of your list. You said that I'd be able to walk and work, but what about love?'

Flushing slightly, Maddy kept her words as clinical as possible as she said, 'You're still physically capable of having sex. I'm sure the doctors told you that.'

West laughed sardonically. 'Telling me—and having it proved, are a world apart. I'd find it impossible with my legs like this.'

'But not if . . .' Maddy stopped abruptly.

'If?' West raised his eyebrows at her. 'Well, go on— Nurse. Don't stop there.'

Maddy took a deep breath, becoming aware of the pitfall before her, and wondering which way West was going to go before he led her into it. 'Not if the—the person you were making love to—helped.'

'Helped?' West was deliberately obtuse. 'Made love to *me*, you mean?' She nodded briefly and he said, 'Ah, I see.' His grey eyes held hers. 'But who am I going to get to help me in this—experiment?' Deliberately he left the question hanging in the air. Maddy tried to drag her eyes away from his but couldn't, tried to make some remark to break the growing tension. But in a battle of wills like this she was no match for West, and it was he who finally broke the silence by saying in a voice of suggestive mockery, 'You, perhaps?'

She let out a long breath. Ought she, she wondered, to be flattered that he'd named her first, instead of Delia? Well, she wasn't, definitely not. Her chin coming up, Maddy said acidly, 'Sorry, but there's a limit to what I do for my salary.'

West flinched, and his eyes grew cold as ice. 'In that case,' he told her curtly, 'you'd better tell Mother to send up a bottle of champagne with dinner tonight.'

For a couple of seconds Maddy thought that he'd only said it out of spite, but there was a grim look about his mouth that frightened her. 'No, West, you can't. It's too soon. You don't have enough strength to...'

'I'll be the judge of that.'

'West, please don't try it. You could...'

'As you've just reminded me, *Nurse*, you're being paid. And I'm not paying for your advice, so just get out of here.'

'You're quite right,' Maddy retorted bitterly. 'You never bothered to listen to my opinions before, so why the hell should you now?' And she strode out of the room, slamming the door behind her.

It was a good hour or so before Maddy could bring herself to go down into the kitchen where Laura was putting the finishing touches to the evening meal. 'Sorry, I should have come down and helped.'

'Nonsense. I'm quite enjoying it.' Laura added a small vase of flowers to the tray. 'There, how does that look?'

'Very attractive.' Maddy said sincerely. 'Our wedding-present lace napkins, too.'

'Oh, dear, do you mind?'

Maddy did, but she shook her head. 'No, of course not. I left them behind for West, anyway. But there are only two trays; aren't you going to join them?' she asked with little hope.

'Good heavens, no. West won't want me playing chaperon.' Laura put a hand to her mouth. 'Oh, that was tactless again, wasn't it? I must remember to watch my tongue. But it's such an odd situation.'

You can say that again, Maddy thought tartly. But it was unlike Laura to be so gauche; usually she was just the opposite and could be relied on to say exactly the right thing. The circumstances must have gone to her head.

But now the older woman frowned and said, 'West has asked for a bottle of champagne with the meal; do you think we ought to let him have it? It's all right for Delia, of course, but West is still on antibiotics and shouldn't drink alcohol, should he?'

'No, but he's going to do it anyway, so why try and stop him?' Maddy answered grimly. But Laura's frown deepened and she said, 'A small glass won't do him any harm, but tell Delia to make sure that's all he has. She'll have to drink the rest.'

'Well, let's hope she has a good head; we don't want two legless people on our hands,' Laura remarked, and then turned in surprise as Maddy broke into almost hysterical laughter.

It took Laura a few seconds before she saw her own joke, and then she too began to laugh, and of course it was just at that moment that Delia chose to walk into the kitchen.

'Hi. Is this a private party or can anyone join in?'

Maddy gasped and began to choke, so it was left to Laura to try and stop laughing enough to say, 'Oh, yes. I mean no. Do come in. What a—what a lovely dress.'

'Thanks.' Delia's voice was dry as she looked from one to the other of them. 'Is there anything I can do?'

'Oh, no, everything's in hand. I've put the hostess trolley in West's room, so once the food is taken up, you'll be able to serve yourselves. Do you like crème brûlée? I've made one for pudding.'

Maddy went to get herself a glass of water and, while she sipped it, looked Delia over. It *was* a beautiful dress. Of creamy-coloured wool that was gathered at the low-cut bodice and hung in graceful folds to where it split above the knee and then fell to her feet, it was an expertly cut creation that more than showed off her already rounded curves. And Delia looked good herself, her make-up perfect and her hair lacquered into a very becoming style.

'Such a pity West isn't well enough to come downstairs yet so that we could all eat together,' Delia remarked, but didn't sound too sad about it.

She helped Laura to carry the food upstairs, but Maddy stayed in the kitchen, preparing their own meal, which she and Laura ate in the dining-room. Maddy chatted lightly over the meal, and it wasn't too difficult to keep her thoughts off West and Delia, but afterwards, when they sat in the sitting-room with

Laura concentrating on her tapestry work while Maddy watched a film on television, it was more difficult to stop her mind from wandering.

The others had finished their meal, of course; Laura had been up to collect the dishes, but the champagne and glasses had stayed up there. But then, it had been quite a large bottle, one of a crate that West had been given after he'd won a race some time ago. Maddy wondered briefly how much West had drunk, but she wasn't too worried about him; he never drank a lot and he definitely wouldn't want to drink for what he intended tonight. 'You'll have to teach me to sew like that,' she said to Laura in sudden desperation.

The older woman gave her a startled look, but said, 'Yes, of course. Why don't you come and sit next to me and I'll show you how I do it?'

So Maddy got through the next hour, although she didn't really learn very much. But then the phone rang just after ten and she went out into the hall to answer it, and as she said the number heard West pick up his own extension.

'Hello, Maddy, it's Tim.'

'Oh, hello. How are you?'

'Fine. Listen, about this afternoon . . .'

Maddy listened for West to put his receiver down, but it didn't come and Tim went on, 'I'm sorry I missed you. I did try to catch you up, but you weren't in the lane and I couldn't see you in the woods.'

'No, I—the dogs chased a rabbit and I had to go after them.'

There was a sound on the line that could have been a snort of derision, and then the familiar click as West at last replaced the receiver.

'Did you get back before it rained?' Tim was asking.

'Er—no, I sheltered under a tree.'

'Well, let's hope it doesn't rain on Sunday when we go to the arboretum.'

Maddy went to speak, but before she could Tim went on, 'You're not free now, are you? I know it's late, but I've just been out on a call and I thought perhaps we could go for a drink for an hour—make up for this afternoon.'

For a moment Maddy was tempted. It would be one in the eye for West, and give him something else to think about. But hardly fair on Tim to go out with him for those reasons. And she was beginning to have a very guilty conscience about Tim, so she said, 'No, I'm afraid not. And Tim—about Sunday; I really don't think it would be such a good idea, after all.'

'But why not? I thought we had a date.'

'Yes, I know, but I've been thinking about it and I really feel that it would be better if we didn't see each other again. Socially, that is.'

'But why ever not? I thought we were getting along very well. Is it something I've done or . . .'

'No,' Maddy broke in wretchedly. 'I'm sorry, Tim, I just don't want to go out with you again.'

'I can't accept that, Maddy. You've got to tell me why,' he protested determinedly.

'Look, I—I don't want to discuss it over the phone. Please, Tim, just try to accept my decision. It's for the best. Truly.'

'No, I won't. I'm going to come round there on Sunday, and even if you won't go out with me, you can at least tell me what's brought this on. You owe me that, Maddy.'

'No, I'm sorry. I—I can't.' And she put down the phone before the note of entreaty in his voice could soften her resolve.

Maddy went back into the sitting-room, but didn't resume her embroidery lesson, instead sitting in a chair and gazing like a moron at the television screen, her mind torn between her own problems and wondering just what was going on upstairs. Not that she cared from an emotional viewpoint, of course, but as a nurse she had a right to be concerned if West tried to over-tax his strength.

At ten-thirty she stood up abruptly and turned off the television. 'Goodnight, Laura. See you tomorrow.'

Her ex-mother-in-law looked up from the magazine she was now reading and smiled at her. 'It's rather early yet, isn't it? Oh, no, I suppose not. Goodnight, my dear.'

Maddy went into her own room and then through the communicating dressing-room to West's door. She could hear music from the cassette-player, slow and smoochy. And then the giggling sound of Delia's laughter, followed by West's much deeper voice. It sounded as if they were having a good time. Maddy gave one hard rap on the door and then marched in.

Delia was reclining on the bed beside West, leaning on his shoulder, her hairstyle not so immaculate now and her face flushed from the wine, a glass of which she held in her hand. Maddy's eyes fell to the bottle and saw that it was under a quarter full. She lifted them and saw West looking at her sardonically. 'Do come in,' he said mockingly. 'Want a glass of champagne?'

'No, thanks.' She went to walk towards him and then stopped. He was wearing the blue silk pyjamas she'd so carefully chosen for him. The rat! Picking up his wrist as if it stank, Maddy glared coldly down at him as she took his pulse, but West only gazed back at her with that taunting look that made her want to kill him. 'How much wine have you had?' she demanded as she let his wrist fall.

'Just enough,' he declared with subtle meaning in his tone, his eyes still laughing at her.

Maddy had been about to warn Delia not to let him overdo it, but she stopped short when she saw that Delia, too, was looking at her with amusement in her eyes.

'Goodnight, then,' she said coldly and walked over to the communicating door. But as she turned to shut it she saw West whisper something in Delia's ear. She giggled and slid off the bed, and the moment after Maddy had shut the door, she heard the key turn in the lock on the other side!

CHAPTER SEVEN

MADDY didn't even attempt to get undressed and go to bed. What would have been the point? She'd never be able to sleep with West entertaining his old girl-friend virtually in the next room. At first she tried to concentrate on other things: tidying her cupboards and drawers, sorting out some clothes that needed to be cleaned. But that took all of ten minutes, and then there was nothing to do but listen to the muted sound of music that came from the next room—and the oc-casional peal of feminine laughter. Then the music stopped and the laughter too, and that was worse. If Maddy had had a radio in her room she would have turned it on, but she made a point of never having one in case a patient called her and she didn't hear. And now it seemed altogether beneath her dignity to go down to the study to get one and turn it on, much as she would have liked to.

For another ten minutes Maddy sat in her room, trying not to think about what that silence meant. But what could *she* do about it? Short of banging on a locked door, there wasn't a damn thing... A thought came to her suddenly and Maddy stood up, her face alight as she wondered if she dared to carry it out. Then she remembered West's taunting eyes and she decided that she could—definitely. Without giving it second thought, Maddy grabbed up her jacket and ran down to the study where she helped herself to a couple of keys from West's desk. Her heart beginning to thump with mischievous excitement, she ran round to the garage and unlocked it, the well-oiled doors lifting easily up into the ceiling. Not that she needed to worry about noise, because Sandy had gone down to have a drink with his cronies at the pub and his windows were unlit.

Maddy found the light switch by the door and a dozen strong fluorescent tubes illuminated the garage as bright as day. There it stood, West's red Ferrari, standing out like a glowing jewel between her old van and Laura's sedate saloon. The car that West would never let anyone but himself drive. Using the other key that she'd taken from West's desk, Maddy unlocked it and slid into the driver's seat, the soft leather upholstery like a sweet-smelling cocoon. Searching around, she found the levers that adjusted the seat to fit her, then turned the key in the ignition, confident that Sandy had the engine tuned to perfection. It fired at once, the engine noise reverberating round the building. With a smile of pure devilment, Maddy turned on the headlights and drove the car out of the garage and round to the front of the house—just under West's windows.

The curtains were drawn of course, but she could see the soft glow of a lamp behind them. Taking the car out of gear, Maddy pushed her foot down on the accelerator, revving the engine in that individual unmistakable roar that could only come from the Ferrari, and which West couldn't fail to recognise. Maddy fastened the safety strap, but kept her eyes on West's windows, waiting for the curtains to move. A light came on in Laura's room, but it was only seconds later that one of West's curtains was pulled back and she saw Delia looking out. There was plenty of light from the porch lamp for the other girl to see the car and give a description of it back to West, not that he needed one. Maddy gave her about a minute, then put the car in gear and drove fast down the driveway, deliberately skidding the powerful machine round the bends. There was a good view on both sides from the driveway into the road and, a quick glance confirming it was clear, Maddy unhesitatingly swung the Ferrari into it and set off along the road, the full, throaty roar of the engine echoing through the night.

Only when she was sure that she was far enough from the house for them not to hear the engine any more, did Maddy slow down and wonder what she was going to do next. She hadn't thought beyond taking the car and getting West as mad as fire. She could imagine his reaction at anyone other than Sandy even touching his precious Ferrari. And he knew as well as she did that Sandy was at the pub. Well, while she'd got the car, she might as well enjoy it, Maddy decided, and headed for the nearest motorway.

To reach it, it was necessary to skirt a couple of towns, and she had just had an exhilarating five minutes on the empty bypass round one of them when she heard the wail of a police siren behind her and realised they they were coming after *her*! Darn! And yet she'd been so careful not to exceed the speed limit. Apprehensively she pulled into the side and the police car parked in front of her, effectively stopping her from driving away. Two policemen got out and one immediately came to her side of the Ferrari and yanked open the door. 'All right. Out you come,' he said brusquely.

A Ferrari is a very low car and somewhat awkward to get out of, especially if you're a woman and wearing a skirt. Maddy couldn't help but show quite a bit of very shapely leg as she obeyed him, and the eyes of both policemen widened in growing surprise and appreciation as she slowly stood before them.

'Ur-hum.' The older policeman cleared his throat and recollected that he was on duty. 'Are you the owner of this car, madam?'

'Well, not the owner, no. But I wasn't speeding, officer,' Maddy assured him.

But he went on, 'And do you have the owner's permission to take it?'

'No, but he can't drive it himself so I thought I'd take it for a run,' she explained helpfully. 'He's recovering from an accident, you see.'

'Is he now? And do you happen to know the number of the car? Without looking, please.' Maddy had known it once, but it had been a long time and she shook her head helplessly. 'I see. Or the name of the owner?'

'Oh, I know that, it's West Marriott, of High Beeches near Aberton,' she answered in some relief.

'The racing driver?' the policeman exclaimed in amazement. Then recovered and said, 'And would it interest you to know that this car has been reported as stolen?'

'Stolen?' Maddy stared at him bug-eyed. Then, 'The skunk! He knows darn well I haven't stolen it, officer. I just went for a ride in it, that's all.'

'Well, I'm afraid that's something we'll have to clear up back at the station, miss. Your name, please?'

'French,' Maddy said shortly. 'Madeline French.' She looked at the policeman disbelievingly. 'Are you really *arresting* me?'

'I'm afraid so. If you'll get in the police car with me, the constable will drive the stolen vehicle back to the station.'

'It is *not* stolen,' Maddy protested as he put his hand on her arm and made her get in the other car. 'And you'd better tell your colleague to be careful, that engine is extremely powerful if you're not used to it.'

The drive to the local police station was short, but Maddy kept turning to make sure the Ferrari was following them safely, even though it would just serve West right if it did get damaged.

At the station she had to suffer the embarrassment of being searched and locked in an interview room for ages before a detective came to take her statement. His eyebrows rose when he saw her, and again when she gave the same address as West's.

'I think it might be an idea if I got on the phone to Mr Marriott,' he remarked.

'You do that,' Maddy agreed, thinking with some satisfaction that at least West's night with Delia had been completely ruined; lovemaking would have been the last thing on his mind when his beloved Ferrari was in jeopardy.

She thought that she would soon be released, but it was nearly another hour before they let her out. Admittedly she hadn't been bored while she waited; two of the younger policemen had brought her cups of tea and stayed to chat, making it plain that they rather admired her ability to handle the Ferrari. 'Wouldn't mind having a go in one of those myself,' one remarked enviously.

West had sent Sandy to fetch her. He greeted her with a frown of disapproval for the benefit of the police, but couldn't hide the fact that he found the whole thing extremely funny. He had to hand over a written declaration from West that he wouldn't be making a complaint after all, and the policeman then handed over Maddy and the keys to the Ferrari. Sandy only said yes, no, and thank you until they were outside the station, then he took another look at her furious face and burst into laughter.

'It isn't funny,' Maddy snapped. 'West had no right to report the car as stolen.'

Sandy laughed again. '*You're* mad? You should have seen West when he realised it was you who'd taken it. Cor, I wouldn't like to be in your shoes when you get back. Here, I came in your van. You can take that and I'll drive the Ferrari.'

Maddy shot him a fulminating glance, but had already come to that unpleasant conclusion herself.

The drive back to High Beeches was a lot slower than the outward one. Lights were on on both floors, although it was now nearly three in the morning. Sandy had arrived well before her and had put the car away in the garage, but had gone to the house to reassure West that it was still in one piece. He was coming down the stairs just as Maddy let herself into the hall.

'The boss wants to see you,' he informed her with a big grin. 'Right away.'

But Laura, still fully dressed, had come out of the sitting-room and said anxiously, 'Are you all right? Oh, Maddy, how could you? You frightened me to death.'

'I'm sorry,' Maddy said contritely. 'I didn't mean to scare anyone. I just—I just wanted to...'

'You don't have to tell me why,' Laura broke in, and then smiled herself. 'But wasn't it rather drastic?'

They're on my side, Maddy thought in surprise. She gave them a grateful grin. 'I'm sorry you've been kept up so late. Where's—er—where's Delia?'

'Oh, she went to her room quite some time ago,' Laura told her. 'I believe West told her there wasn't any point in staying up. And now that you're safely back I shall go to bed, too. Goodnight to you both.' And as she passed Sandy, 'We haven't had so much excitement in ages.'

Maddy saw Sandy out after thanking him for coming to collect her, and then made sure the house was securely locked before going upstairs herself, switching out the lights as she went. She felt in a strange mood, her former anger and indignation lost under Sandy's mirth and Laura's understanding. It felt odd to have them on her side when they had always been on West's before. But then, this was only a small and trifling thing to them—even if it wasn't to West. As Laura had said, Delia's door was firmly closed, but West's stood open—and she had to pass it to reach her own room.

'Maddy!' He was sitting up, on the watch for her. 'Get in here. I want to *talk* to you.'

She hesitated in the doorway. 'West, it's late and I...'

'Damn you, you don't take my car and then sneak off to bed,' he snarled. 'I want an explanation.'

'Do you?' Still in this odd, detached kind of mood, she came into the room and shut the door behind her. 'What do you want to know?'

West frowned, expecting her to be belligerent and surprised by her tone. 'Why you took the car, for a start?'

'No, you don't. You already know why.'

'But I want you to tell me, all the same,' he ordered, his eyes fixed on her face.

Maddy gave a shrug and sat down in an armchair, kicking off her shoes and tucking her feet under her. 'All right. Because you goaded me into it. You made me jealous and I couldn't stand the thought of you and Delia—together.'

West's eyes widened. 'Coming from you, that's quite an admission.'

'Yes, interesting, isn't it?' she agreed.

'Have you been drinking?' West asked suspiciously. 'You don't seem your usual argumentative self.'

'Don't I?' She laughed. 'Sorry, I'm not in the mood.'

'Or are you just trying to distract me?' West guessed, his face hardening. 'Let's get back to the car. Where did you go after you did your ruining-the-engine act under my window?'

Maddy smiled. 'I knew you'd be worried to death about the car. I drove past Aberton and out towards the motorway. But I . . .'

'You got that far?' West stared at her. 'In a car with a three-point-five-litre engine that you'd never driven before?' he said in an appalled voice. 'Do you realise what could have happened?'

'Yes, of course,' she said shortly. 'I might have put a dent in your beloved Ferrari. Though why the hell you should care when you'll probably never drive it again I...'

'I was worried about *you*, damn it!' West snapped. 'How could you have been stupid enough to take it when all you're used to is a broken down old van that won't go over thirty miles an hour?'

'I haven't always had the van,' Maddy objected. 'And besides...'

'OK, so you had a decent car while we were married, but nothing like the power of the Ferrari.'

'That's right, you always made sure I had a very sedate car, didn't you?' Maddy remarked pensively. 'Almost as though if I had anything more powerful I might get the urge to race—like you,' she mocked. 'And somehow I don't think you would have liked that.'

West gave her a baffled look. 'You never liked speed.'

'You never gave me the chance to find out.' She gave a secret kind of smile. 'So *I* decided to find out.'

West leaned forward, his body suddenly tense. 'What are you saying?'

Maddy didn't answer for a moment, enjoying having him guessing, but soon relented to say, 'Merely that when you and Sandy were abroad racing, I took the Ferrari out. Often.'

'You couldn't have,' West exclaimed. 'You couldn't handle...' He stopped, remembering how far she'd driven that evening. Then his face hardened. 'You're lying,' he said crisply. 'Sandy and I would have known from the mileage.'

She shook her head, a smile playing on her lips. 'I paid a garage mechanic to show me how to put the mileometer clock back.'

'Why, you little...' West leaned back against his pillows, convinced at last. 'And did you find that you enjoyed driving fast?' he grated.

'Yes, I enjoyed it,' Maddy admitted, 'but not because I was in a hurry to get from A to B. I enjoyed the feeling of power under my hands, of having that huge engine at my command. I felt that I wanted to put my foot hard down and really go.'

'But that's how...' West was staring at her. 'That's how I feel sometimes when I race.'

'Yes, I imagined it was.' Her face shadowed and Maddy swung her legs down and stood up. 'I think that when I realised that I couldn't go on fighting you any more. Oh, it took me a while to admit it to myself, let alone to you, but that's when I knew me and my silly dreams would never be able to compete against racing.'

'Your dreams?' West's eyes were fixed intently on her face.

'Yes. When I finally admitted to myself that they would never come true with you, I was very practical and told myself I must leave you so that I could have a chance of meeting someone else and finding happiness with him.'

Some of the colour had gone from West's face, and there was a pinched look about his mouth. 'And is that what you've been doing—searching for someone else?'

Maddy shook her head and gave a laugh that was strangely close to tears. 'It's the silliest thing, but once I was free I found that my dreams could never come true anyway—because you were the only one whose...' She broke off abruptly and headed for the door.

'Maddy, wait!'

She stopped and slowly turned to face him, her eyes over-bright. His eyes asked the question and she answered it as if he'd spoken. 'You know what I wanted. I wanted to hold our child in my arms.'

West's jaw tightened and a pulse throbbed in his neck. 'I offered to let you start a family,' he grated harshly.

Maddy smiled sadly. 'So you did. But what were you willing to offer other than helping to conceive it?'

'What do you mean?'

'I mean that I wanted a real father for my child, one who was going to be more than a scrapbook of Press cuttings and a row of trophies on the sideboard!' Her voice had risen, but she bit it off abruptly, aware of the other people sleeping in the house. She gave a self-reproachful shake of the head. 'I'm sorry. I—I had no right to say that now. And I'm sorry I took your car. I...'

'Oh, for God's sake stop being so meek and humble,' West cut in brusquely. 'You had as much right to expect what you wanted from the marriage as I did. I'm just sorry that it didn't work out the way you wanted.'

'Now who's being humble?' Maddy smiled. She came to stand beside his bed and looked sadly down at him. 'I suppose it was just—just irreconcilable differences, exactly as they said in the divorce petition.

No one's fault. Just another mistake that had to be put right.'

'But there was always love,' West said softly, and reached out to take her hand.

'Yes,' she agreed, 'there was always that. It's a pity it wasn't enough.' His fingers tightened for a moment, but West was silent, until after a few minutes Maddy said, 'And you, did you try to find someone—someone to take my place?'

Slowly, West lifted a hand and brushed her cheek. 'No. No one could do that.'

She gave a half-disbelieving smile. 'Not even Delia?'

West's face darkened. 'When I want a woman,' he said forcefully, 'I'll do my own lovemaking.' But the anger left him as he continued to look at her, and then his hand slipped behind her neck and he pulled Maddy down to kiss her very tenderly.

When she lifted her head, Maddy's eyes were wet with tears. She tried to say something, but was too choked up and could only manage an uneven, 'Goodnight, West,' before she ran into her own room.

Everyone slept in the next morning, making up for the late night. For Maddy it had been even later as she'd lain in bed, feeling a weight of unhappiness that was nearly as great as when she'd first left West almost two years ago. Sleep had come slowly, drifting in on waves of sadness that were so poignant that it was driven away again, until tiredness conquered at last.

Breakfast was a patchy and stilted meal, with everyone eating at different times. Maddy came down to find that she was the first in the kitchen, and just had a glass of orange juice while she cooked Laura's breakfast, intending to take it up to her, but then

Sandy came in and he ate Laura's toast. He stood watching while Maddy made some more, and it was obvious that he was dying to know what had happened between her and West last night. Maddy didn't enlighten him, of course, so when West's buzzer sounded Sandy hurried upstairs, hoping to get more out of him. Five minutes later he came down again, looking a bit put out, and stole Laura's breakfast again to take up to West.

Laura eventually got her breakfast, but not until she had come downstairs herself. She was just finishing it in the breakfast-room opening off the kitchen, and Maddy was having a cup of coffee with her, when Delia came in.

'Oh, good morning. I do hope you—er—slept all right,' Laura said awkwardly.

'Sure. Fine, thanks,' Delia answered with a polite smile.

Maddy stood up. 'I'll get you some breakfast.'

'No, no. You finish your coffee,' Laura insisted. 'I want to talk over the weekend menu with Mrs Campbell.' She turned to Delia and said diffidently, 'I do hope you'll be staying with us for the weekend.'

'I'm afraid not. I have to get back to the friends I'm visiting with. In fact, I wanted to order a car to take me to the station. If you could tell me the number I'll . . .'

'Oh, that's quite unnecessary. Sandy will be happy to take you.' Realising what she'd said, Laura added hastily. 'That's if you're sure you won't stay. You're most welcome to . . .'

'Thanks, but I have to go back.'

Laura nodded and went out of the room, leaving Maddy to break the awkward silence that followed by saying, 'I'm sorry. I've spoiled your visit.'

'That was the idea, wasn't it?' Delia remarked shortly.

'Yes,' Maddy admitted, 'I suppose it was. But it wasn't your fault, and it was hardly fair to—to involve you.'

'I gather it was West who did that. He wanted to make you jealous. And he certainly did that.'

To Maddy's relief Delia didn't seem very mad at her, a bit short but not angry, so she smiled as she nodded. 'Yes, I'm afraid so.'

Delia looked at her contemplatively. 'But there was really nothing to get jealous about, was there?'

'Wasn't there?' Maddy gave her a direct look. 'You and West were lovers once.'

Delia hesitated a moment, then nodded. 'Yes, we were, but that was years ago, before he even met you.'

Her eyes on her coffee-cup, Maddy said slowly, 'But West has been back to America more than once since—since we split up.'

'So that's what you're thinking. West never even looked me up. If he had—well, I'd have been more than willing.' She looked steadily into Maddy's eyes which were fixed intently on her face now. 'That's why I came here in such a rush when he called me. But it soon became quite clear why he'd invited me, and I told him off for it. But as the poor guy explained, there's not a lot he can do himself when he's tied to a bed like that. So I went along with it. But that wasn't what I meant when I said you had nothing to get jealous about.'

'No? I got it wrong? What did you mean, then?'

'I meant that it was quite clear that West is still in love with you. And by the way you reacted, you're obviously in love with him, so why hack at one another like that?' She looked at Maddy's lowered head. 'You do know that he's in love with you, don't you?'

Maddy brushed a hand across her forehead and nodded. 'Yes,' she admitted huskily. 'I know. But we—we just can't live together.' She got quickly to her feet. 'I'm sorry, Delia, but I really can't discuss it.'

'Well, maybe you ought to try—with West.' She gave a crooked smile. 'I'm not the only female on the lookout for a man like him, you know. Be careful you don't lose him completely.'

Maddy managed a smile but shook her head, knowing that she'd lost West long ago, and was glad to escape when Laura came into the room carrying Delia's belated breakfast.

Delia had left by the time Maddy went up to give West his physio session, and neither of them mentioned her, or what had passed between them last night. Instead they concentrated fixedly on West's exercises, extending the time by another few minutes, and as he put intense effort into them, he looked a little grey and exhausted by the time they finished.

'Have a good rest before this afternoon's session,' she cautioned him. 'You mustn't overdo...'

'I won't,' he cut in shortly. 'What are you doing this afternoon?'

'It's my turn to go into Aberton and take the library books back. And I have one or two other things to do.'

'Like having lunch with Tim Roberts?' West demanded grimly.

'No.' She shook her head, hesitated, then said, 'I—I told him I don't want to see him again.'

'When? When did you tell him that?' West's eyes were suddenly fixed on her face.

'Last night. He...'

'You saw him last night?'

'No, he rang. You heard him. You picked up the extension.'

He nodded. 'And what did he say when you told him?'

'That's nothing to do with you, West. I don't...'

'Isn't it?' It was said intently, not angrily, and she realised that she could be open with him now, that they had got beyond the stage of jealousy and distrust. For a moment she felt closer to him even than when they were married.

'He wasn't very happy,' she admitted.

'No, I don't suppose he was.' West picked up her hand and held it for a moment, then gently carried it to his lips to kiss her ringless fingers. 'He knows a good thing when he sees it.'

Maddy's hand trembled convulsively, then she quickly took it away. 'Well, I'd better get going,' she said briskly. 'Have a good rest.'

She was half afraid that she might see Tim in Aberton, but she kept her shopping to a minimum and was back within a couple of hours, not having seen him. She was afraid, too, that he might ring again, but he didn't, and by Saturday afternoon she had become hopeful that he had accepted her decision and wouldn't come round as he'd threatened.

But early on Sunday afternoon the doorbell rang and he stood on the doorstep.

'Hello, Maddy.' It was a windy day and he was wearing jeans and a padded jacket, making him look somehow different from when he wore his usual dark suit. Like a soldier who had put on civilian clothes.

'Hello, Tim.'

She gave him a rather helpless look and he said, 'I'd like to talk to you for a while, if you can spare the time.'

'Tim, I'm sorry, but I . . .'

'Just for ten minutes,' he insisted. 'This is your coat, isn't it?' He stepped into the hall and took her coat from the peg, held it for her to put on.

'I *can't*. I'm sorry, but I . . .'

'Yes, you can. West can spare you for ten minutes.'

Reluctantly Maddy obeyed him, realising that he had made up his mind and wouldn't go away until she agreed. But she put her head in the sitting-room and said to Laura, 'I'm just going out for a few minutes. I won't be long. If—if West should ask— you'll tell him. Just a few minutes.'

'Yes, dear, I'll tell him,' Laura agreed calmly.

Maddy had expected they would go for a walk, but Tim opened the door to his car and she got in uneasily, wondering where he was going to take her. But he drove for only a few minutes before he drew up in a lay-by near an area off the main road that had been set out with picnic tables, a green place cut off by trees from the noise of the traffic.

'Let's walk, shall we?'

They got out of the car and Tim came round to join her. He stood still, looking at her troubled face, then said shortly, 'I believe I owe you an apology. I—inadvertently—made some unkind comments about you?'

Maddy frowned for a moment, not understanding, but then remembered the remarks Tim had made about 'West's wife'. 'You know, then?'

'Yes. I happened to mention you at the Drama Group and a woman there knew you. She—enlightened me, and rather enjoyed doing it,' he added grimly.

'Tim, I'm sorry. I . . .'

'Why didn't you tell me?' he broke in. 'Why let me find out that way?'

She shook her head. 'I don't know. I've been using my maiden name ever since the divorce.'

'But you could have told me that you're West's wife!'

'I'm *not* his wife. We've been divorced for nearly a year.'

'So why are you living at the house now? Why *you*?'

'Because no one else would take on the job of nursing him. You know how the other nurses left,' Maddy exclaimed.

'I know how West *made* them leave. Was that so that you would have to come and nurse him?'

'No! No, that wasn't it at all. Laura was desperate. She couldn't get anyone else,' Maddy told him.

'So he needed you. And you came—even though you were divorced.' Tim looked at her. 'So you must still feel something for him.' He turned and walked a few steps, then swung round to face her again. 'Is that why you said you didn't want to see me any more?'

She nodded. 'Partly. But also...' She paused, trying to pick words that wouldn't hurt him. 'You seemed to—to like me. To want to get involved. When you told me about that job at the hospital, I began to feel—scared.

'Scared? Of me?' Tim asked in amazement.

'Not of you, no. But of what you wanted from me. Tim, please try to understand; I've just been through a marriage that has failed and I'm trying to pick up the pieces again. I don't want to be pushed—to get involved in another relationship so soon. I need time to find myself again.'

He frowned at her broodingly for a moment, then said. 'It doesn't make any difference to me, you know, that you've been divorced.'

'Thank you,' Maddy said sincerely.

'But that doesn't mean anything to you, does it?' Tim said wryly. 'Because you're still in love with West.' Maddy nodded silently and he gave an exasperated sigh. 'But I heard that *you* left *him*. Are you hoping West will take you back, is that it?' Maddy still didn't answer and he said, 'Oh, I know it's none of my business. I just wish to hell it were.'

'I'm sorry,' Maddy repeated, feeling helpless and guilty. 'It's my fault, I should never have gone out with you.'

'No, never say that.' Tim came closer and put his hands on her shoulders. 'Meeting you has been—quite something. You're a very wonderful girl, Maddy. And I hope you—find what you're looking for.' He hesitated. 'But if it doesn't work out—if you and West don't get back together...'

'I know.' Maddy lifted up a hand to touch his face. 'I won't forget—and I won't forget *you*.'

He nodded, then went to lightly touch her forehead with his lips before he quickly stepped away. 'I'd better take you back—I don't want my patient to have a relapse.'

Maddy half expected West to cross-question her about Tim when she got back to the house, but he took one look at her set face and wisely refrained. He didn't even mention Tim's name, but when the doctor came on his normal weekly visit the following Wednesday, West's eyes were fixed on them both intently when Maddy showed Tim into the room. But whatever he saw—or perhaps the lack of anything to see—reassured him, and he bent all his energies on getting well.

Maddy helped him all she could, of course, but sometimes she felt as if she was taking part in some sort of macabre ritual, a merry-go-round of fate in which they both strove to make West well, knowing that he was going to go back on the race track and risk his life all over again. Like a wounded soldier being made whole to go back to the war. Only West, of course, had a choice; he could retire and no one would think the worse of him. He had been driving in Formula One races for eight years now and had been very successful, not only in racing but in the business interests that had grown out of racing. He didn't need the fame and he didn't need the money, so why not do the sensible thing and quit while he was still, more or less, in one piece? But Maddy had come to accept that he couldn't, not yet. Whatever compulsion drove him to race still wasn't spent, and maybe it never would be, maybe he would just keep on racing until... Maddy's mind recoiled from the obvious conclusion. Grimly she went on doing her best to make him walk, and shut her mind to what would happen when he could.

They worked so well that, one afternoon about a week or so later, Maddy went into West's room with a tape measure in her hand. He was lying on top of the bed, apparently having fallen into the sudden tired doze of an invalid that still sometimes overcame him. He was lying on his back, so Maddy was able to spread out her tape and measure from his feet up towards his armpit.

'Measuring me for my coffin?' West asked drily.

Lifting her head, Maddy saw that he had opened one eye and was looking at her lazily. 'No, for a pair of crutches,' she answered evenly. 'It's about time you got out of that bed and started getting yourself around.'

West's eyes widened and he looked at her intently. 'Haven't you heard?' he said in a flippant tone that couldn't hide the tension. 'I can't walk.'

'In that case, I might just as well measure you for a coffin, mightn't I?' Maddy returned as she straightened up.

Lifting his hand, West caught her wrist as she began to rewind the tape. 'When?' he demanded unsteadily. 'Today?'

'No. Today all you're going to do is to try to stand up for a few seconds.'

He gave a sudden harsh laugh. 'How can I possibly walk if I can't stand on my own two feet? Of course I can stand up.'

Maddy laughed. 'You'll be surprised.'

And he was, more than surprised, when later that afternoon, with Maddy and Sandy on either side of him and Laura watching anxiously, he tried to stand up for the first time in nearly six months. He was worrying more about whether his legs would hold him, and wasn't ready for the waves of dizziness that made him hastily sit down on the bed again after only a few moments.

'It's all right,' Maddy said quickly. 'You've just lost your sense of balance. It will soon come back.'

He looked at her, greedy for reassurance, and received it from her steady gaze. 'OK. Let's give it another go.' And this time he managed to stand for a few seconds longer.

He would have gone on if Maddy hadn't called a halt, but as his balance returned, so did his determination to walk again once West was sure that his legs would hold him. But Maddy wouldn't let him use the crutches to do more than stand, even though he wanted to try, until his Harley Street surgeon had seen him and more X-rays had been taken. Only when the surgeon had given his approval did she allow West to take his first step.

'Well?' he demanded impatiently when she came back to his room after phoning the surgeon. 'What did he say?'

'He said that your legs have mended well and evenly. You shouldn't have a limp, although you'll probably be half an inch or so shorter than you were before.'

'Really?' West looked surprised, then shrugged. 'So what's half an inch when you're over six feet anyway? But what did he say about my trying to walk?' he repeated eagerly. 'When can I start?'

'We-e-ell...' Maddy looked at him under her lashes, teasing him.

'Maddy, for God's sake!'

'All right.' She smiled at him. 'How about today?'

His eyes widened, and then filled with such a look of relief and hope and joy that Maddy had to quickly turn away to fight the lump that came into her throat. 'I'll get Sandy,' she said tightly.

Laura, of course, came too, and it became a repeat performance of the first time that West had tried to stand. 'OK,' Maddy cautioned. 'Take it easy. Don't try to rush things. And remember how I told you to distribute your weight.'

West nodded impatiently and pulled himself up on to the crutches, stood there for a moment as he gathered himself. 'All right, you can let go,' he grated, his mouth pinched because it still hurt like hell.

Slowly Maddy let go of his arm and moved to stand a little way in front of him, so that he could take only a couple of steps and she could catch him if he fell. She nodded to Sandy, and he too let go. West's brow creased in intense concentration, his teeth gritted against the pain, but he gripped the crutches and slowly moved one leg forward, but wobbled so that Sandy made to grab him.

'No! Leave me alone.' Beads of perspiration stood out on West's forehead as he forced bones and muscles to work again and tried to drag his other leg forward. His eyes lifted to meet Maddy's and their gazes locked, West's challenging and determined, almost as if he was taking his strength from her. Slowly his leg came forward and he took a step, put his weight on it, and stood still. Laura and Sandy began to clap and cheer, but West's eyes, full of blazing triumph now, still held hers. 'I did it!' he yelled. 'I knew I'd damn well show you I could. Now I'll walk again—and I'll race again too.'

Maddy found that silly tears of relief were running down her face, but his last words made her breath suddenly catch in her throat. She tried to say something but couldn't, could only look once more at the towering happiness in his face—then turned and ran out of the room.

CHAPTER EIGHT

AFTER that first, sweet taste of success there was no holding West back. He gradually used the crutches more and more each day. He was still having his physiotherapy sessions too, and now Maddy also began to massage his legs and hips more, a time that she both loved and dreaded. She tried very hard to be professional and clinical, but she only had to touch his skin to be filled with the most tender memories. So often in the past, when West was feeling tense, he had asked her to give him a massage, and they were always so sexually aware of one another that it had led to making love nearly every time. In fact it had become part of their private language; West only had to flex his shoulders and look at her and she knew exactly what he meant. And at times she thought that West remembered too; when his hands curled into tight fists, when his body grew stiff with tension instead of relaxed, when she lightly stroked and massaged his skin.

Neither of them spoke about it, of course, and there was little time left to even think about it. West was working so hard that Maddy had to take the crutches right out of his reach to make him rest at all. But he improved every day, and by the time Maddy's birthday came round could get himself out of bed and round his room and the bathroom quite easily.

When she awoke that morning, Maddy lay awake for a while, thinking of other birthdays in far happier times, but then got up briskly, dismissing the memories; this, like last year's, was a birthday she wouldn't be celebrating. But in that she was wrong, because when she came down to breakfast there was a little pile of cards and a parcel by her plate. The room was empty for the moment, but Maddy stood looking down at the cards without touching them, wondering if she wouldn't rather have had the occasion forgotten.

'Happy birthday, my dear.' Laura came bustling in and gave her an affectionate kiss on the cheek. 'I've made you your favourite breakfast: kedgeree and freshly squeezed orange juice.'

'You shouldn't have gone to all that trouble,' Maddy protested.

'Nonsense. Birthdays are special. Aren't you going to open your cards?'

The top few cards were from her family and long-time friends, but underneath there was a card from Sandy and supposedly from the two dogs, which made her laugh, and under that a card from Laura. It was the last one in the pile. 'Thank you,' Maddy said sincerely. 'It's a lovely card.' She hesitated and then slowly reached out to pick up the small, square parcel.

'That's from me, too,' Laura told her.

With steadier fingers, Maddy untied the wrapping and opened a little box. Inside, between layers of cotton wool, was an antique brooch in the shape of a butterfly, worked in diamonds and lapis lazuli. Maddy's eyes widened and she gave a little gasp. 'But Laura, this is one of the pieces your grandmother left you. Surely it's the René Lalique brooch?'

'Yes,' Laura admitted. 'But I want you to have it.'

'Oh, but I couldn't. It's much too valuable.' And Maddy put it back in the box and tried to give it to Laura.

But the older woman shook her head. 'And haven't you given me back something far more valuable? Something that I can never repay?'

'You mean West. He would have got well again, Laura, I'm sure of that.'

'Well, in that I think we'll have to disagree. But please take the brooch, Maddy. As a very small token of how much I appreciate what you've done for West. It will give me very great happiness to think of you wearing it.'

'Thank you. I shall—treasure it always,' Maddy accepted stiltedly, still reluctant, but knowing that to refuse further would offend Laura. 'And I'm glad that—that everything has worked out as you wanted it.'

'Oh, I think things might even work out better than I'd dared to hope,' Laura answered with a teasing smile.

Maddy merely thanked her again, her tone non-committal, and ate her breakfast slowly, putting off the moment when she would have to go up to West.

'I wonder if you'd mind going into town for me later today?' Laura asked. 'I promised to collect old Mrs Allinson from her sister's at six-thirty, but now I find I won't have time. She goes to have tea with her sister every Wednesday, if you remember.'

'Why, yes, but . . .'

'Oh good,' Laura said before Maddy could protest, and she got quickly to her feet to carry out a stacked tray.

Maddy gave a resigned sigh; she didn't particularly mind collecting the old lady, but the timing precluded her from going to the cinema as she'd planned. Still, what did it matter? Any other day would do just as well.

West was sitting in the armchair by his bed, having got himself into a track suit. He looked so different from when she first came, Maddy thought. Then he had been so gaunt and thin, his eyes haggard. But now his face had filled out and looked just as lean and hard as it had always done, and his old, indomitable will was back in his grey eyes.

'You're late,' he said abruptly. 'You should have been here ten minutes ago.'

Maddy smiled with inward self-mockery; so much for worrying about having to face him on her birthday; West hadn't even remembered. But at least it meant that there wasn't any awkwardness between them and she could carry on as if it was just a normal day. But, unusually for him, West declared himself tired at five o'clock, so Maddy had an hour in which to phone her family and drop a line to her friends to thank them for her cards. At six she drove into Aberton in Laura's car to pick up Mrs Allinson, a nice old lady who insisted she say hello to her sister and then, when Maddy had taken her home, come in to see the latest piece of exquisite needlepoint tapestry that she was working on.

So it was gone seven-thirty before Maddy got home. She hung her coat in the hall cupboard and went to go upstairs just as Laura put her head out of the kitchen door and called, 'Dinner in about half an hour. I knew you'd be in a hurry, so I've put a dress out for you.'

'Oh! Thanks,' Maddy answered in surprise, but her eyes opened even wider when she went into her room and saw the dress that Laura had chosen. It was a full-length evening dress in soft shades of blue and grey, with a very full skirt that swirled from the hips, a quite low-cut bodice and long, tight sleeves. A designer dress that Maddy had almost forgotten because she hadn't taken it with her when she'd left West. It must have been in a cupboard somewhere and Laura had found it. Maddy fingered the soft material, remembering the first time that she'd worn it—then cursed herself for a fool. She had to put the past behind her, to forget it. The future was what mattered. But that wasn't true either; the future stretched only into emptiness, and she quickly pushed that aside too as she went into the bathroom to shower and change.

Laura must have invited a guest and forgotten to tell her earlier, Maddy decided as she put on the dress. It was a little too big—she'd lost weight since she'd bought it—but she still looked good in it, and she automatically did her hair up in a more sophisticated style and put on more than usual make-up. When she was ready, Maddy stood and looked at herself in the full-length mirror with the strangest feeling of *déjà vu*. It was almost as if she'd gone back in time to when she was still with West, still the wife of the famous racing driver. Wearing it was a mistake, she realised that at once, and she wanted to tear off the dress, and pull down her hair and wash her face. But the half an hour was more than gone and Laura hated to have dinner kept waiting. But then, what did it matter? Maddy realised as she went downstairs. After all, she was the only one who would notice, or would care.

The door to the drawing-room stood ajar and Laura called out, 'We're in here.'

Pushing the door fully open, Maddy walked into the room—and then stopped in stunned surprise. The room seemed to be full of flowers, and they were predominantly her favourite, roses, which were on every table and shelf, their scent heavy on the air. But what held her eyes was West. He stood—he actually stood on his own two feet without crutches—in the centre of the room, dressed in a dark evening suit and looking so—so like the old West that Maddy could only stand and stare at him.

He grinned, pleased that his surprise had been so successful, and said, 'Happy birthday, Maddy.'

Thoughts rushed in incoherently: that he shouldn't be standing without his crutches; that he looked so damned attractive; the flowers were the same as those in her bridal bouquet and he usually sent them only on anniversaries; no, it was OK, Sandy was standing near enough to catch him and grinning like a Cheshire cat; there were so many flowers; and, oh, God, West, why have you done this when you know I have to leave you?

'I'm afraid I'm kind of stuck here,' West said, 'but if you'd like to come closer I could give you a birthday kiss.'

Slowly, unresistingly, Maddy moved towards him. Her eyes were on his face, but as he reached to put his hands on her arms she closed them and stood waiting, every sense concentrating on his touch. His hands tightened for a moment and then she felt his lips brush her cheek. 'Maddy, I . . .'

His words died and she opened her eyes to find him gazing down at her intently, a strangely helpless look on his face. But then he leant forward again and kissed her firmly on the lips.

Maddy flushed and pulled quickly away, which sent West off balance. In the laughter as everybody made a grab for him, she was able to regain a little composure, but her cheeks were still flushed as West was given back his crutches and they went into the dining-room to eat.

Between them Laura and Mrs Campbell had cooked a banquet of a meal, and the housekeeper had stayed on to serve it. There was watercress soup, smoked salmon, a delicious main course of chicken supreme, and to top it all a birthday cake with twenty-seven candles. There was wine throughout the meal, too, and a bottle of champagne with the cake.

'Now, you must remember to make a wish when you blow out the candles,' Laura instructed. 'And I hope it comes true for you, my dear—whatever it is you want.'

Maddy smiled and hesitated, trying to think. But there were so many things she could wish for, and none of them now could ever come true. She shook her head a little, her eyes suddenly sad, and glanced up to find West watching her frowningly. Quickly she smiled and blew out the candles, made a joke about the number that made Laura and Sandy laugh, but didn't deceive West for a minute.

To wipe out that moment of bleakness, Maddy drank quite a lot of the champagne, but was aware of West watching her, a glass with only mineral water in it in his hand.

The party ended at eleven when Maddy noticed that West was looking tired after his first time downstairs. She and Sandy watched him up the stairs, and Sandy helped him to bed while Maddy said goodnight to Laura and went into her own room. As she reached up to undo the fastening of her dress, Maddy caught sight of herself in the mirror again. She looked flushed and excited, almost young again, she thought hazily. Because tonight had been so different from what she'd expected. It had been a wonderful birthday, one that she would remember always. And the most wonderful part had been that West hadn't forgotten. He must have denuded every florist's shop for miles around to find so many roses. Impulsively, Maddy went downstairs again and brought up one of the vases of flowers, putting it on the little table beside her bed, so that it would be the last thing she would see tonight and the first thing in the morning.

She undressed and put on a robe before going into West's room. 'You OK?' she asked.

There was just his bedside lamp on, and by its light she saw that he looked very tired and more than ready for sleep. He turned to look at her and reached out a hand to take hers. 'Yes, fine. You?'

'Of course. Thank you—for tonight.'

West gave a small smile and carried her hand to his lips, a gesture that was so familiar it made her heart turn over. 'What did you do on your last birthday?'

Maddy's thoughts went back to a year ago. 'Nothing very much,' she said dismissively.

Perhaps there was something in her voice, because West looked at her more closely. 'Tell me,' he insisted.

'It really isn't very edifying.' But West's raised eyebrows and the thrust of his jaw told her that she wasn't going to get away with it that easily, and she sighed. 'I was working. An elderly man had broken his hip and I was looking after him at his house in Gloucester. He had a son, about forty, who was staying at the house. This son, he saw me opening my cards at breakfast and he insisted on taking me out that evening, although I didn't want to go. I don't have to tell you the rest, do I? He wanted paying for his supper, and got nasty when I refused. I couldn't stay on, not while he was there. I left the next day.'

She had been looking down, but now she lifted her head to look at West, saying lightly, 'Just one of the perils of being a working girl.' But her voice died as she saw the blazing anger in his eyes.

'Who was he?' He demanded tightly. 'I'll kill the bastard.'

'West, for heaven's sake! It was over long ago. I don't think I could even remember his name now if I tried. And anyway, men think they have a right to make a pass at the nurse. It's an occupational hazard. You said that yourself,' she reminded him.

'You must give it up,' he said fiercely.

'You know I can't do that.'

'You could if you'd accept the money I offered you,' West countered. 'But you're so damn proud and stubborn.'

Maddy laughed. 'I'm fine. Don't worry about me, I can take care of myself.'

'You shouldn't have to fight men off.' His hand balled into a tight fist as he gripped the coverlet. 'I can't bear to think of you being pawed and handled,' he said harshly.

'West, don't. Please. Look, you're tired. I'll go so that you can get some sleep.'

She went to move away, but West caught her hand again. 'You can stop me helping you, but you can't stop me worrying about you—or caring.'

'No, I suppose not,' she agreed on a sigh, but then her voice hardened. 'It seems that we're both stuck with that.' Firmly she took her hand away. 'Goodnight, West.' And she went quickly from the room before they could torment each other further.

But although Maddy was tired herself, sleep didn't come for some time. Up until now she had been able to think of West as a patient, but seeing him tonight downstairs in a natural environment had been totally unnerving. He was himself again now, masculine, vital and forceful. And now there was no holding back the immense physical attraction she still felt for him. And it had been so long since he had held her in his arms and loved her. Maddy stirred restlessly, her body hot and aching.

In the end she gave up trying to fight, letting the memories wash over her until sleep came at last. But in the early hours she began to dream, a horrific dream of West taking part in a race in which she knew he was going to crash. She was running towards the pits, desperately trying to warn him, but her legs felt like lead and no matter how hard she tried she couldn't go any faster. She began to call out to him, to scream at him not to go, but she could see West getting into his racing car and beginning to drive out to the track. She screamed his name again, knowing that he was going to be terribly hurt, her mind bursting with terror.

'Maddy! Maddy, wake up.'

As she came out of the terrible nightmare Maddy was totally confused for a moment, unable to recognise which world was real, the dream had been so vivid. But then she saw that West was standing over her, balancing on his crutches as he shook her shoulder. She gave a great cry of relief and sat up, her head in her hands, her body still shaking with fear. 'Oh, God! Oh, God.'

'It's all right. It's over now.' West sat awkwardly down on the low bed and put his arms around her, holding her and rocking her back and forth like a child. 'It was only a dream, sweetheart.'

Maddy shuddered and clung to him, the sweat of terror still on her skin. 'It was so real. I really thought you were...' She broke off, and drew a little away from him. 'I'm sorry, I woke you up.'

'I thought something terrible had happened to you.' West looked at her flushed face. 'And I was right. It must have been some nightmare.'

Maddy nodded and leant back against the bedhead, out of his arms, another tremor running through her. 'I'm OK now.'

'You don't look it. What was the dream about?'

'What?' Maddy put a hand up to her head again. 'Oh, I don't remember.'

'Yes, you do. It was about me, wasn't it?' She didn't answer, and he went on heavily, 'You'd better tell me, Maddy.'

But she shook her head. 'It doesn't matter. It was only a dream.'

'But real enough to make you scream for me.'

Her eyes widening, Maddy lifted her head to look at him. 'Did I? What did I say?'

'Just called my name and shouted ''Stop'' and ''Don't''. So it doesn't take much imagination to guess what you were dreaming about. Was I racing?'

Maddy hesitated, but then nodded. 'Yes, they're always about racing.'

'You've had them before?' he questioned sharply.

'Oh, yes,' she answered bitterly. 'I used to get them a lot—when you were racing. Never when you were home. But I'd thought I'd got over them since—since I left.'

'You never told me.'

Maddy gave a harsh laugh. 'As I said, I never had them when you were home. If I told you, would you have believed me? You'd probably have thought it was just another ploy to make you give up racing.'

West didn't speak for a moment, a withdrawn look in his face, then said shortly, 'You're right, I probably would have done. I came to see your wanting me to give up as a battle, and I was determined to win. But the battle became a war and I was so busy winning I didn't realise that I'd lost until it was too late.' Reaching out a hand, he gently pushed a damp tendril of hair off her cheek. 'I didn't understand, did I?'

'You didn't even try,' Maddy returned with a short, sad laugh. 'You just expected me to be the same as all the other girls who ran after you, willing to follow you all over the world and to live for racing. Well, maybe I was like that at first, starry-eyed and over-whelmed by the glamour of it all, but the glamour wore off and then there was only the man I loved risking his life over and over again until I couldn't bear it any longer!' She stopped abruptly and said in little more than a whisper, 'I'm sorry. That was—un-necessary. I must have had too much to drink, it's made me maudlin.'

'Or truthful.'

She shook her head. 'You'd better go back to bed, West. Thanks for coming in to me.'

'Any time.' His brooding grey eyes looked into hers for a moment, then he put a hand behind her head, drew her to him and kissed her. It was a kiss of deep tenderness, without passion, but full of warmth and feeling, an embrace that enveloped her soul, making Maddy feel as if there was no other world but this closeness, this exquisite joy of his lips on hers.

They drew apart at last and Maddy was aware of an aching void of loss. She looked away, unable to meet West's eyes, and said quickly, 'Can you manage to get up? Shall I help you?'

West didn't answer for a few seconds, but she still didn't look at him, and eventually he said in a tight voice, 'No, I can do it.' He heaved himself up. 'Good-night, Maddy.'

'Goodnight. If I have another nightmare just throw a jug of cold water over me.' And she turned away, facing the opposite wall to the door, her heart beating as she listened to him going over to the door and closing it carefully behind him.

Only then did she give a soft moan and bury her face in the pillow, her body doubling into a tight ball as if she was in physical pain. She lay like that for a long time, and when daylight crept into the room had forced her unwilling heart to accept that the time had come when she must go, she must leave West now all over again. Only this time was going to be a million times harder even than the first.

The next morning Maddy was up early despite the sleepless night, and got busy on the phone as soon as she could. Her first call, strangely enough, was to Tim Roberts and was a little difficult, but he gave her the information she wanted so that she was able to make the second, and now very important, call. To her relief, this worked out just as she'd hoped, which left her free to take down her suitcases and start packing. This done, she went downstairs to see Laura.

After greeting the older woman, Maddy asked if she could borrow Sandy for an hour or so.

'Why, yes, of course. Did you want him to work on your van?'

'No. But I wanted him to put my physio equipment into it. I'm leaving today, Laura.'

'But why?' Laura turned to stare at her. 'After last night . . .'

'Last night proved that West doesn't need me any more. He'll soon be as good as new again. Nothing can stop him now. You have no need to worry.'

'It's not that.' Laura stood hesitating, her face troubled. 'But you and West—I hoped . . .'

'I only agreed to come until he was well again.'

'But even so. Surely you've grown close and...'

Maddy walked quickly to the door. 'No. If you'll excuse me. I'll go and find Sandy.'

'Have you told West?'

'Not yet. But I'd rather tell him myself, Laura.'

'Yes, of course.' The older woman still looked stunned. 'But how will West manage without a nurse and without physio treatment?'

'Don't worry, it's all taken care of. You know I wouldn't leave him stranded.'

She escaped to the garage, but had to go more or less through the same conversation again with Sandy before he came back into the house with her and began to take her equipment downstairs. Then she went in to West.

'What's going on?' he demanded at once as she closed the door behind her. 'What's Sandy doing?'

He was wearing his tracksuit again and was standing over by the window, looking down at where she'd parked her van outside. 'Is there something wrong with your Interferaction machine?'

'No, there's nothing wrong with it,' Maddy replied steadily. 'Sandy is putting it in the van for me, that's all.'

She went to go on but she didn't have to. West said in a grim, abrupt voice, 'You're leaving.'

'Yes. I've arranged for you to have physiotherapy from the man who looks after the local football team. Tim said that he's by far the best around here.'

'Tim Roberts? So he knows you're leaving.'

'Yes,' Maddy acknowledged, adding, 'I said goodbye to him.'

'And now you've come to say goodbye to me.'

'Yes,' she said again.

'But why?' West swung himself over to her. 'Why today? Why so suddenly?'

She smiled. 'Last night you came in and looked after *me*, so I realised that if you're well enough to do that, then you certainly don't need me any more. Now you can get yourself downstairs, Sandy will be able to take you for treatment in the car. You'll be fine.'

West made an impatient gesture. 'That isn't what I meant and you know it. I want you to stay. And you want to as well. You said that you still loved me.' His voice became forceful, urgent. 'Stay, Maddy. Be my wife again.'

She shook her head, fighting back tears. 'I can't, West. Yes, I love you, but . . .'

'And I love you.' He caught hold of her arm, a crutch falling unheeded on the floor, and gripped her tightly, as if he would make her stay. 'Maddy, darling, I owe you so much. Don't leave me again. Not again. I want you. Can't you see that?'

'West, don't. I have to go. I must, I . . .'

But he pulled her roughly to him and kissed her fiercely, his mouth taking every opportunity as he sought to dominate and bend her to his will. For a few moments Maddy surrendered, thinking how easy it would be to give in and have this always, but then she drew back, holding him off with her arms.

'No, West. You know I can't stay. Unless you're willing now to give up racing?'

'No, not yet. I . . .' He seemed about to say something. But then shook his head. 'I'm sorry, I have to race again.' But he said it with true regret, and at least Maddy knew that he understood.

'You see,' she said trembling. 'Nothing's changed. So you must let me go, West. And don't make it hard for me this time. If you owe me anything, you owe me that.'

She picked up his crutch and gave it to him, took one last look at his white, tense face, then went into her room, picked up her cases and went out to the van where Sandy and Laura were waiting. She said goodbye to them and the dogs, but didn't look up at West's window again before she got into the van and drove away.

At Christmas Maddy received cards from both West and Laura; West had just signed his name, but with Laura's there was a little letter telling her how well West was getting along, that he was still on crutches but was living a more or less unrestricted life. Laura sent another letter a couple of months later which was forwarded on to Maddy at another nursing job. In it Laura said that West was using only a stick now and most of the time managed without it. After that Maddy didn't have to rely on letters, she read in the papers of West's miraculous recovery and his immediate return to driving. It was reported that he was practising as much as possible with a view to taking part in the first Formula One race of the season.

Those words brought an iciness into Maddy's heart that nothing seemed to melt. The family she was with were nice people and would have treated her as part of the family, but she began to withdraw into herself, much as she had done after the divorce, and she spent many hours alone in her room. The date of West's

race came round and luckily coincided with the end
of that assignment, her patient back on her feet, so
she was free to go back to London and be by herself
without having to pretend any more. But on the afternoon of the race she couldn't stay in, she had to go
out and walk aimlessly through the streets and the
park, looking in windows whose contents didn't regis-
ter, gazing at flowers she couldn't smell.

At five o'clock she heard a church clock chime and
knew that it would be over. She turned and hurried
now to where a man was selling evening papers at a
news stand. She took some money from her purse and
joined the small queue of people waiting to be served,
her coat collar up against the chill wind. The line
moved up, much too slowly for her, but then she froze
as she saw the headline written in large capitals on
the placard at the front of the stand. 'Marriott Wins
Comeback Race'.

Somebody behind jostled against her. 'Are you
buying a paper or not, miss?'

'What? Oh, no. Sorry.' Blindly she turned away,
thanking God that West was safe but wishing that he'd
lost, lost so completely that it would have dis-
heartened him. But now that he'd won, she knew that
nothing would stop him from competing in top-class
racing. He would be travelling all over the world again,
living the life he loved, risking everything until . . .
Maddy pushed that thought aside and let herself into
her flat. The phone was ringing, but she let it go on
until the caller gave up, and then she took the phone
off the hook; she was in no mood for sociable chats
tonight.

She didn't turn on the television or radio, or bother to get herself anything to eat, instead putting a cassette into the player her parents had given her for Christmas. It was rather sad music, telling of a love found and lost, and it more than suited her mood. It made her cry—she told herself it was the music—and tears ran down her cheeks and slowly dried there when the music stopped, and she still sat on.

The sound of the doorbell broke into her reverie, making Maddy jump. She sat up, looking at her watch, and saw that it was nearly nine. She almost didn't go to answer it, but then thought it was probably her neighbour who was always running out of things, and reluctantly got up and went to the door.

'Hello, Maddy,' West said as she stared at him in stunned amazement. 'May I come in?'

She didn't answer but he came in anyway, his eyes taking in the unhappiness in her face, the dark shadows around her eyes. He walked ahead of her along the tiny hall and into her sitting-room, looking round, taking everything in. 'So this is where you're living.' He turned to face her. 'I've often wondered what it was like. Tried to picture you here.'

'Is that why you came?' she got out in a strangled, gasping voice. 'Were you—were you passing?'

He looked amused. 'No, of course not.'

'Then why... I don't understand why you're here?' she said in distress.

'Don't you?'

'No, I . . .' She stopped and her face tightened with tension. 'If you've come here to thank me for getting you well enough to win that damn race . . .'

'So you know I won?'

'Yes.' Maddy's hands balled into white-knuckled fists. 'I saw the announcement on a placard.'

'And that's all you saw? You haven't been watching the television?'

'No.' She gave a puzzled frown. 'Why should I?'

But West glanced at his watch and said, 'It's almost nine, let's put the news on.' And he walked over to the television set and switched it on.

'What is this? West?'

'Shut up and watch,' he commanded in a tone that she recognised only too well. But then he grinned at her and put a chair in front of the set. 'Here, you'd better sit down.'

'But I . . .'

'Quiet.' He put a hand on her shoulder and pushed her down on the seat. 'Watch.'

'Look, I don't have to take orders from you,' she began belligerently, and turned round in the chair to look angrily up at him, but what she saw in his face made her breath catch in her throat and then turn wonderingly towards the screen.

West's race was the third news item. It showed the start and then West overtaking other cars, once absolutely brilliantly, going through a gap no car had a right to even contemplate, to take the lead and hold it. It showed the crowds going wild and the commentator's jubilant voice as he did a lap of honour. Maddy began to turn to him again in puzzlement, but he put his hand on her shoulder and said, 'Watch again.' The next shot was of the podium and the usual prize-giving with champagne spraying everywhere, but then there was a close-up of West as he spoke into the cameras. He began by thanking all his fans who'd wished him well, his racing team for giving him this chance to drive again, 'And most of all' he added, 'I want to thank my physiotherapist for convincing me that I could walk again and getting me back on my feet so quickly.'

So that was it, Maddy realised, he wants me to know that he's expressed his gratitude in front of everyone. Well, what more did she expect? A sharp pang of disappointment filled her, but before it could start to hurt West began to speak again and she gave her attention to the screen.

'This has been a doubly momentous day for me,' West went on. 'Winning this race after being away so long has made a very wonderful climax to what is my last day of racing. I had determined to take part in one more race and I am now equally determined to give it up completely, to retire and hopefully to pick up my family life again. A task that will be far harder but far more rewarding than any race I could ever take part in.' He said goodbye and then turned to shake hands with the men from his racing team. The commentator made some more remarks about his past successes and then it went on to another item. It was all over. He had receded into the past as quickly as that.

For a while Maddy didn't move, and West came to turn off the set and then squat down in front of her. 'Maddy?' he said anxiously. She turned her wide, astonished eyes to his and he said quickly. 'I had to prove to myself that I could do it, that I hadn't lost my nerve. If I hadn't, I wouldn't have had any respect for myself. Can't you see that?'

'Why didn't you tell me?'

He gave a helpless kind of shrug. 'In our circumstances—I couldn't. I had to do it alone.'

'I see.'

'Do you?' He rose to his feet and pulled her up with him. Softly he said, 'You made me a whole man again, Maddy. Except for one thing.' He smiled down at her. 'I need a wife.'

She was suddenly angry. 'You louse! I've been going through hell these past weeks. I ought to refuse to marry you.'

West's mouth twisted as he tried to hide his laughter. 'But Maddy, I need a wife *very* badly.'

She looked at the dark need in his eyes and blushed. 'That much, huh?'

'Definitely.' His lips found her temple and went insinuatingly on down to her throat, making her give a low moan of awareness.

But before she succumbed completely, Maddy said huskily, 'Hey, you remember that bet we had? I never claimed my prize.'

His eyes came up to hers, an arrested expression in their grey depths. 'Have you decided what you want?'

'Mm. Do you . . . If you've still got them, could I have my rings back some time? I miss them so.'

West looked at her lovingly, but then reached into his pocket. 'It so happens...' And he slipped the rings back on to her finger. 'And no giving them back again,' he said on a note that contained a remembered hell.

Maddy smiled mistily. 'No, no giving them back.'

'Good.' He kissed her in growing passion, but at length said thickly, 'Now that we're as good as married again, can we...?' He gestured towards the bedroom.

Maddy laughed happily up at him and let him take her hand. 'I guess every winner deserves a prize.'

West led her into the bedroom and shut the door. 'Well, this is a battle you've certainly won,' he smiled a little ruefully.

'No.' She put her arms around his neck. 'We've both won.'

He looked down into her radiant face and smiled. 'Maybe we have at that,' he agreed.

Harlequin Presents

Coming Next Month

1199   THE ALOHA BRIDE   Emma Darcy
Robyn is at a low point in her life and is determined not to be hurt again. Then she meets Julian Lassiter Somehow she finds herself wanting to solve Julian's problems in a way that is not only reckless but is positively dangerous!

1200   FANTASY LOVER   Sally Heywood
Torrin Anthony's arrival in Merril's life is unwanted and upsetting, for this shallow, artificial actor reminds her of Azur—the heroic rebel sympathizer who'd rescued her from cross fire in the Middle East Could she possibly be mixing fantasy with reality?

1201   WITHOUT TRUST   Penny Jordan
Lark Cummings, on trial for crimes she's innocent of, hasn't a chance when she is faced with James Wolfe's relentless prosecution. Then the case is inexplicably dropped. She wants to hate this formidable man, but finds it impossible when fate brings him back into her life!

1202   DESPERATION   Charlotte Lamb
Megan accepts a year apart from her newfound love, Devlin Hurst—she'll wait for him. Yet when her life turns upside down just hours after his departure, she knows she must break their pact. Only she has to lie to do it.

1203   TAKE AWAY THE PRIDE   Emma Richmond
Toby lies about her qualifications to become secretary to powerful Marcus du Mann—and is a disaster. But when Marcus gets stuck with his baby nephew, Toby is put in charge. And she's coping well—until Marcus decides to move in and help....

1204   TOKYO TRYST   Kay Thorpe
Two years ago, Alex walked out on Greg Wilde when she discovered he was unfaithful. Now they're on the same work assignment in Japan. Despite Greg's obvious interest in the beautiful Yuki, Alex finds herself falling in love with him all over again!

1205   IMPULSIVE GAMBLE   Lynn Turner
Free-lance journalist Abbie desperately wants a story on reclusive engineer-inventor Malacchi Garrett. Then she discovers the only way to get close to him is by living a lie. But how can she lie to the man she's falling in love with?

1206   NO GENTLE LOVING   Sara Wood
Hostile suspicion from wealthy Dimitri Kastelli meets Helen in Crete, where she's come to find out about the mother she never knew What grudge could he hold against a long-dead peasant woman? And how would he react if he learned who Helen is?

Available in September wherever paperback books are sold, or through Harlequin Reader Service:

In the U.S.
901 Fuhrmann Blvd.
P.O. Box 1397
Buffalo, N.Y. 14240-1397

In Canada
P.O. Box 603
Fort Erie, Ontario
L2A 5X3

You'll flip . . . your pages won't!
Read paperbacks *hands-free* with

Book Mate • I

The perfect "mate" for all your romance paperbacks

Traveling • Vacationing • At Work • In Bed • Studying
• Cooking • Eating

Perfect size for
all standard
paperbacks,
this wonderful
invention
makes reading
a pure pleasure!
Ingenious
design holds
paperback
books OPEN
and FLAT so
even wind can't
ruffle pages —
leaves your
hands free to do
other things.
Reinforced,
wipe-clean vinyl-
covered holder flexes to let you
turn pages without undoing the
strap . . . supports paperbacks so
well, they have the strength of
hardcovers!

Pages turn WITHOUT
opening the strap

SEE-THROUGH STRAP

Reinforced back stays flat

Built in bookmark

BOOK MARK

BACK COVER
HOLDING STRIP

10 x 7¼ opened
Snaps closed for easy carrying, too

Available now. Send your name, address, and zip code, along with a check or
money order for just $5.95 + 75¢ for postage & handling (for a total of $6.70)
payable to Reader Service to:

Reader Service
Bookmate Offer
901 Fuhrmann Blvd.
P.O. Box 1396
Buffalo, N.Y. 14269-1396

Offer not available in Canada
*New York and Iowa residents add appropriate sales tax.

BM-G